JOHN SPEKE, PISTOLMAN

by
Lee F. Gregson

Dales Large Print Books
Long Preston, North Yorkshire,
England.

British Library Cataloguing in Publication Data.

Gregson, Lee F.
  John Speke, Pistolman.

  A catalogue record for this book is
  available from the British Library

  ISBN 1-85389-820-1 pbk

First published in Great Britain by Robert Hale Ltd., 1997

Published in Large Print 1998 by arrangement with Robert
Hale Ltd.

Dales Large Print is an imprint of
Library Magna Books Ltd.
Printed and bound in Great Britain by
T.J. International Ltd., Cornwall, PL28 8RW.

JOHN SPEKE, PISTOLMAN

Ruthless and powerful Jeb Cady made a bad mistake when his battered wife Harriet left him to seek help from her sister. Cady hadn't banked on the appearance of Meg's consort—John Speke, a renowned pistolman. Though Cady sent men after Harriet, Speke stepped in and took one of them back, slung across his horse, dead. When Cady stalled for time, Speke discovered as nasty a can of worms as could be imagined. He had fraud and murder to investigate and it would prove to be his toughest and most dangerous challenge yet.

ONE

By some small miracle the letter had caught up with them in a town called Slane.

Meg was sitting on the edge of the rumpled bed and, having slipped on her lightweight, cream robe, had taken the single sheet of paper from the envelope. After a few seconds she said, 'It's from Harriet.'

Sluicing water out of a china bowl over face and neck, then drying off with a white towel, his suspenders hanging on either side of his pants, Speke half turned his large face to her, but he said nothing until, slowly, now reading, she murmured, 'It's written from Denton. She's in Denton.'

Drying his bold, droopy black moustaches, then his hard hands, he did turn

5

around now, his dark eyebrows lifting. 'What the hell's she doing in that place?' Though he was affecting only minimal interest as he asked the question, Meg did wonder, and it had to be admitted not for the first time, about that. Speke hung the towel on a rail at the end of the wash-stand, slipped a shirt on and lifted the suspenders, shrugging them over his wide shoulders.

'John, she's left Jeb; come right away from Sabina on account of that.' Meg looked closely at the torn envelope. 'This was mailed ten days ago.'

'Then maybe she's not in Denton any more.'

'She says she's got no plans right now except she's not going back to Sabina.'

Speke was buttoning his shirt and still, she thought, covering real interest with a mundane preoccupation. Meg sat there, the letter now held in her lap. Still a good-looking woman, small, shapely, with dark hair that at this early hour was clouded

6

around her narrow shoulders, watching out of her dark eyes the man's familiar movements. 'I think it's help she needs.'

A metal-backed brush in either hand, he was stroking at his thick hair that he wore centre-parted and bunching thickly at his neck.

'She say that?'

'No.'

Now he glanced at her. 'Sixty miles, Denton. An' not the way we're headed.'

Outside, the dry, hot wind had got up again already. The sash-cord window was partly raised and the creased, brown-stained blue shade was moving stiffly, an acorn-sized pull rattling on the sill.

'If it wasn't help that she was really wanting she wouldn't have written. Not this one page that says a lot and says nothing. From where she's alone.' In all probability, he thought, this was true. Younger than Meg by seven years, as a girl Harriet had been unfailingly cheerful, spirited and independent. Marriage to Jeb

Cady had cured her of that, but not, they had both believed, to the point at which she could no longer go on with it. Meg said, 'I should have kept in closer touch with her, all through, not just now and again.' Self-accusation, this. But accusation that was intended to widen to include Speke? Probably. He thought so, anyway. An apportioning of guilt. After all, it had been Speke who had first brought Cady on the scene, all of them younger then; Speke, in his youth, readier to accept Cady's darker side, to be easy on him because of other, counterbalancing things. Yet at the time, even using the excuse of youth, Speke had not given it enough thought, not realizing, at least to begin with, that Cady's busy eyes having lighted on Harriet Rawlins, would find in hers an instant and warm response. So, by then it was too late anyway. Meg asked, 'So, what do we do?' Maybe he had already made up his mind and was only being drawn out slowly for the sake of appearances.

'I guess it's not so far, at that.' Which meant that they would go.

'I really think we should, John.'

'We'll go.'

With one of her narrow white hands she reached out and touched him on a hand. She knew how much he wanted to move on, get shut of this place where they had paused to pass a couple of days, and move well away from this part of the country. Indeed, if Harriet's letter had got as far as this just a day later, it would have needed to coat-tail them for at least another eighty-odd miles. Yet she had felt certain, no matter how he had received the news, that Speke's instincts would be to—in a sense—immediately throw an arm around Harriet if there was a chance that that was what she most needed. Then she wondered why it had sprung into her mind in just those terms.

Speke might well have been concerned chiefly for Harriet's welfare but he was sure giving plenty of thought to Jeb Cady, too, and this of course gave rise to other thoughts, cameos held in the mind ready for such a review, some of the memories good, others bad. More than that: some, very bad indeed. Like those associated with the Hepburn posse. Even after all this time, Speke almost shook his entire frame getting rid of those particular images.

'Get dressed, Megs. Time to eat. I'll go down to the livery, see about the horses. Be back in around fifteen minutes.'

The rooming house had a thick, sour smell that they had become aware of as soon as they had set foot inside. Now, in the poorly lit room, Harriet in the narrow, brass-ended bed, Meg standing near, Speke, having knocked, came back in, hat in hand.

'There's still but two hotels in this town,' he said. 'We've got rooms at one of 'em. I've put our baggage there.' Baggage. Hardly worthy of the name. All they could manage to carry on the horses.

10

And as though to deflect any possible argument, Speke added, 'Harriet, you can't go on staying in this dump.' To Meg, he said, 'Call me when Harriet's ready.' He went out.

When, with Meg's help, Harriet had got up and dressed and put on a brown, hooded cloak, Meg opened the door and Speke came in and without saying anything except, 'I'll come back here, after, for your baggage,' scooped Harriet up in his long arms as though she weighed nothing at all; like some farmer rescuing a small animal from a snowdrift.

Walking in through the lobby of the Alonquin Hotel, carrying the woman, Speke gave his gimlet stare to the clerk whom he had earlier paid for their rooms and from whom he had got keys.

'The lady...uh...she's sick?' Nothing had been said to the clerk about sick ladies, and he was now mindful of the possibility of disease spreading through the house. At the same time, this big, moustached man seemed the wrong kind to argue with. And the clerk thought that there had been an oddly familiar echo coming off the name *John Speke*. But whatever it meant, the clerk had so far been unable to make any connection.

'The lady is not sick, she's exhausted,' Speke said in his deep, no-nonsense voice, and without pausing, headed for the stairs. 'C'mon, Meg.' Their shadows were flung large and grotesquely onto faded, stripy wallpaper as they went on up.

Once Speke had got Harriet installed in her room he left the two women there and walked back to the rooming house to fetch Harriet's things. By the time he came tapping at the hotel room door Harriet was again in bed and pleased that it was a cleaner one than she had been in earlier.

Speke, in an unusually soft voice, said, 'We can talk in the morning, Harriet, if you'd rather wait.'

Harriet, pale and sunk-eyed though she was, shook her head slightly. 'No, don't go.' Meg sat down on the side of the bed holding one of her sister's hands in both of hers. Speke sat on a straight-backed chair nearby and dropped his stiff-brimmed hat on the carpet.

She had come as far as Denton, Harriet told them, her once lively violet eyes clouded, and had found that she had no option but to pause there in order to take a long rest, leaving her room only occasionally and indeed moving very slowly when she did, to eat at a café. A growing problem was that she did not have much money with her and therefore she must use what she did have sparingly. By the time Speke and her sister arrived, her funds had all but vanished. Clearly, something was badly wrong to drive her to these extremes.

Now that they were able to look at Harriet properly, in brighter light, they could see that what at first had appeared as a darkening of the skin beneath her eyes, of the kind sometimes produced by sickness or persistent lack of sleep, had taken on the appearance of something more sinister. Harriet then said something that only Meg could hear, and Meg began easing the bedclothes down as far as Harriet's stomach, and with the woman's somewhat clumsy co-operation, raised the nightdress until it was bunched beneath her breasts. In a very tired voice, Harriet said to Speke, 'Don't go, John... Look...'

Meg glanced around at Speke who stood up and came to the bedside and at once his black eyes narrowed. The silken, ivory skin of Harriet's flat stomach and all around her ribs was darkly blotched, discoloured in a dozen places, some of the marks obviously made recently, while others, with a browner tinge to them, were older. Slowly, showing signs of an aching stiffness, Harriet struggled over onto her side, facing away from them. Above the swell of her small, rounded buttocks and narrow waist were other markings, the results of kidney punches.

Speke's big face was like a mask carved out of teak. Presently he straightened up.

'Cady.' It was no question.

'Yes...' No more than a whisper. Gently Meg helped her sister cover herself, then drew the bedclothes up. Meg said, 'My poor love. It's been going on for a long time.'

Lying back against plumped-up pillows, Harriet raised one long-fingered hand slightly, then let it fall. 'It's not quite as simple as it seems; and maybe, to you, what I'm...going to say will sound foolish. Stupid. But there *have* been good times. Truly. It hasn't always...been so bad. John, you must know...what I mean by that. You know Jeb...'

Speke could understand perfectly what it was she felt she had to try to explain to them, for he did well know the strange, often conflicting layers that went to make up the personality of Jeb Cady. He was and had always been a man of resolute but restrained manner—as long as things

15

seemed to be going his way. But whenever he thought they were not, it was a vastly different matter. If Cady felt threatened, and especially if he had been thwarted, he was soon seen to be a man capable of sudden and fierce temper who was more than ready to strike out. A man of moods, was Cady.

'I know,' said Speke, his thoughts going back years.

Taking her time, pausing frequently, in a hushed voice, Harriet told them her story. Some of it they knew already but they allowed her to talk, recognizing that this act of unburdening was a part of what this woman needed as much as she needed rest and kindly care.

She said that the early years of her marriage had in fact been all she could have hoped. It was true that it had been her money that had helped Cady get his start, but it was equally true that they had prospered through the application of his sharp mind and his inherent business

16

acumen. Land had been acquired, and later, some sound business enterprises, these in anticipation of a railroad that one day would indeed find its way up through the Sabina River territory. Jeb Cady had sure turned out to be the right man in the right place at just the right time. There could be no argument but that they had both benefited from that.

Speke now had to ask, 'So, what went wrong?' For it had been a year or two since he and Meg had been anywhere near Sabina and Harriet and Jeb Cady.

'What went wrong?' For several seconds Harriet closed her eyes, then lay with her head fully back, staring at the fly-specked ceiling. 'Just...greed, I guess... power...money and power together.' She slid her gaze down to Meg and Speke. 'Things that have...gone on in Sabina... especially over the past year. Some things that couldn't stand too close a look...you know. Deals, land deals mostly...I know two families were forced off. Both times,

Jeb, he must have had a lot to do with that. He's...the real power there now, in Sabina County Did you know...amongst all of the other things, he's even...the town marshal and I have to say...he's got some very hard men around him. Boothby, the county sheriff...he's a weak man, I think. If it came to the point...he'd never stand up against Jeb...'

It was Meg who asked, 'But what about the people who live there? It's not the small town that it was once, is it? Surely—'

'Meg, you might believe you know what he's like. But did you ever...really know him? I mean, as well as John knows him? He can be pleasant, likeable, he can be...a charming man. God, don't *I* know that to be true? There are lots of folk in Sabina who'd even back him for governor...if he nodded and lifted an eyebrow at the notion. People like them...probably outnumber the ones who'd gladly see him dead. He's strong...a decision-maker. I think that appeals...'

Speke could readily understand that, too, but it was Meg who came back to what must now be seen as the greatest irony.

'It was the money that *you* had, that *you* took into the marriage that gave him his first chance. Harriet. You know it, I know it and so does John.' By no means a fortune but enough, well handled, and Jeb Cady, to give him his due, had surely done that.

'What exactly was it that happened, that first went wrong between you and him,' Speke asked, lifting a hand a little to indicate what he had been appalled to see on her body, 'to bring you to...this?'

She could have said, perhaps, *'No children,'* but that reason had been dwarfed by others. 'Not keeping...my place. Not keeping still. Wrong things said at the wrong moment...sometimes small enough things in themselves...but enough to set him off. You know, not *everything* has gone his way right off. So there were times when

I couldn't be quiet about things I'd heard and...I'd seen. One of the families that had to go...put out by the bank...I'm sure was because Jeb and the banker, Soderman, were working together. And that family, they were such good people. They deserved a better deal.'

'And you said as much?'

She nodded slowly, then smiled, but it was in the bleakest of ways. 'Oh, afterwards he came looking for forgiveness. I mean, for what he'd...done to me. In his rage. I was just stupid enough...to give it. So things went on...even got a little better for a time.' She drew in a shaky breath. 'Then one day...a particular wagon come in...a man and woman and child. They'd travelled more than five hundred miles on the strength of a scrap of paper, title to land they'd paid over their savings for. A farm block down on the Sabina, near Calley Flats. It turned out there was no such block...I mean, not going for sale. And Boothby, of course, and others, could show proof of that. The people were devastated. They had nowhere to go...well, not to stay. They'd all but...run out of money. I truly believe that Jeb pushed others into moving them out...on some pretext.'

'But they'd *paid* somebody for land. Who, and where?' Meg asked.

'Way up in Brooks County somewhere, so I heard...I don't know who. The title looked genuine. I've got a terrible feeling that Jeb...knew a whole lot more about it than *we'll* ever know for sure. And those people haven't been the only ones. But this man...this last man...he was so angry, so...desperate, he swore he'd go back up into Brooks County, get there somehow, near to broke as he was, and get to the truth of it. When I made a fuss Jeb flew into an old-style rage, hit out at me. That was when I made up my mind to leave, go anywhere. Away from Sabina. Away from *him*. But the chance...didn't come right off. Before it did, a man came looking...for that wagon family. The woman's brother... He said he'd come a long way to meet them...help them work their land. On his way he'd come through Brooks County and he'd not seen a hair of them there...or anywhere along the trail...'

'Maybe they'd changed their minds,' Meg said uncertainly.

After a moment or two Harriet said, 'Maybe. We...Jeb and I had another falling-out over it.' Her voice went trailing away. Then, 'That was it... I just couldn't take any more.'

'Does he have any idea where you've gone to?' Speke asked.

Her voice was low, husky. 'I hope not; God, I hope not. He'll not be able to abide the thought of me wandering the countryside the way I am. An out-of-town wagoner got me as far as Rachman. I managed to get on the stage out of there but when I got as far as Denton, I just couldn't go...any further.'

Meg asked, 'Do you really think Jeb will try to find you?'

Again Harriet raised a limp hand, let it drop. 'Maybe. Yes, I'd say he'll try to find me...send somebody looking, maybe. He does have men he could send. It's been nearly two weeks, I know...and they wouldn't know which way I'd gone. But they could still come.'

'And you'd go back with them?' asked Meg.

Harriet moved her head slightly. 'If I said no, what would it mean? I'm tired. I'm sick to death of it all...but I'd have no choice but to go back.'

Speke went pacing slowly away, came back, his mask-like face unreadable. Meg took one of Harriet's hands.

'You're *owed* by Jeb Cady, love. After what's happened he can have no *claim* on you. You're due money from him, *your* money at the very least, more if there's any justice in this world. You don't have to take this kind of treatment, not from

Jeb Cady or anybody.'

'Please...please Meg. I can't even think straight. Let me sleep for a while now...'

Meg patted her hand, tucked it beneath the covers, and turning to Speke, asked, 'Well, what do we do?'

TWO

The Hepburn Posse

It was in a real bad place at the mouth of a canyon in an arid stretch of broken country about eighty miles south-west of Gabriel that it all turned to shit. In choking dust, under the hammering of gunfire at least two of the saddle-horses were down and screaming and one of the pack-animals was loose, lolloping heavily away, disappearing into the grainy murk.

Speke could hear Hepburn's voice yelling, 'Git down! Git down!' but for the moment could not see where the hell the marshal was. For Speke, however, it was enough to make sure that the three prisoners were got down off their head-tossing, screwing-around horses, and try to find some cover for him and for them. Closer to him another posseman, the frequently complaining Pardoe, was also out of the saddle and was now trying to hold onto his horse, the reins tautened, the animal white-eyed, spooked by the eruption of gunfire and the confusion and yelling, pulling Pardoe along jerkily as it went rearing, backing off, Pardoe cussing it savagely. Plenty to complain about now. Thick dust clouded both man and animal.

Through this same swirling dust came Hepburn, towing his own sorrel, shouting some names now, giving them his voice to rally to. 'Cady! Speke! Girdler!' Then, seeing Speke, asked, 'Where's Coverdale? Where's Dryden an' Besant?'

Hobbs was there now. 'Dryden's been hit, Girdler an' all! Lost sight of 'em, after!'

'Jesus!'

'Look out!' Hobbs yelled. 'Here the bastards come ag'in!'

Of all those who were involved in this shambles, Jeb Cady showed up well. Mindful of the extreme danger but by no means cowed, he had discarded a rifle that had developed a fault in the lever action. Now he arrived without his horse, to crouch near to Speke, an old, long-barrelled army pistol in his hand, dust clinging to his clothing and plastered on his sweating skin, aiming, swinging the pistol, tracking a wild-riding figure going plunging through the dust, the pistol bucking, the target swallowed up. Gone. Cady knew he had not hit the man.

They were a hell of a mixture, these attacking horsemen, some of them ragged white renegades like these three they had got hold of, some Mexicans and at least two who, though wearing elements of US cavalry uniforms, were Apache. The three here under Speke's pistol were kneeling, manacled separately, not looking so Goddamn' sparky now, it being evident to them that with all this lead flying they were just as likely to stop some as anybody else.

When for the space of a few seconds the dust thinned sufficiently, just before the riders came hammering back again, Speke glimpsed one of the posse crouching behind a downed horse and thought that it was Dryden; but whoever it was, there was something badly wrong with him. Then the dust thickened and the wild horsemen were thundering through it no more than eighty feet away, and a prolonged Apache yell was going up, a sound to make the neck-hair bristle.

'Goddamn' Ay-pach!' Besant this, arriving rifle in hand, his mount long gone, dragging its ass-end. And he had other information. 'Pack animals is all gone! Cut 'em out, the bastards!'

Cady was shooting regularly as though merely practising with bottles lined up on a fence, and once he called out that he thought that he had hit one of the riders. Somebody unseen had begun a hideous

28

yelling, the sort of sound produced by fiery pain, then Dryden came stumbling across their line of vision—such as it was—his hat gone and the top of his head bald and a bright red mess, scalped, and a lot more wrong with him besides, for rushing away into the murk, the last they saw of him he was reaching up with both hands towards something that only he could see, going back to where the fallen horse was.

Hepburn knew that there was nothing he could do for Dryden, but called out that he was going to try to find where the others were. 'So watch out fer who it is, comin' back in, afoot.' He went, almost at once being swallowed up by the dust. Cady thought that Hepburn's going out like that was a big mistake, and said so. Besant fired his rifle, levered another round in, waited, shot again. Only two or three minutes after that, a thudding sound came. Once...twice.

'Christ!' called Besant, sweat-soaked, plastered with white dust, 'Shotgun.'

Somebody out there yelled, a sound that turned high-pitched, like the sound of some sorely hurt animal. Lead was whipping in, disconcertingly close. Out in the boiling dust a horse screamed. The worst thing was that they did not know where everybody had got to, for the dismemberment of the posse had occurred with appalling suddenness and a great deal of noise.

As it turned out it had been Hepburn himself who had been shotgunned. At first, as they saw him come blundering back through the swirling dust they did not recognize him or see exactly what was wrong with him, but there did seem to be a grotesque distortion to the shape of his body. He was hunched over, staggering, hands clutched to his mid-section. And indeed it was his belly that was all wrong; but it was not until he stopped abruptly before sitting down hard only eight feet from them that they could perceive the dreadful stomach wound he had taken, and suspended from it, bulbously, dark and glutinous, part of Hepburn's intestines. He was making a repeated sound, *'Huh! Huh! Huh! Huh!'*, his body spasming with each eruption of noise. But then he said something like 'Got...' He seemed to be intent on getting the slippery mess back inside his stomach but he was never going to succeed.

On hands and knees Speke went to him. With a monumental effort, Hepburn, his eyes staring, managed to say 'Got... Coverdale.' Speke assumed he meant *shot*. That was not the case but it would be a little time yet before they would discover it to be quite wrong. To Cady and Besant, Speke called, 'Going on out an' have a look. Watch for me.' Pistol in hand, moving in a crouching run, he left them and the dying Hepburn and headed away into the murk.

Eighty feet out he went down on one knee. Across to his left he could just see the shape of a fallen horse with the blood-headed Dryden now lying against it, unmoving, as though listening for the animal's heartbeat. Angling away again, then kneeling once more, hearing the rushing of horses coming, Speke then saw the loom of mounted men going by, shooting, more to unsettle those of the posse still alive than with much hope of seeing clear targets. But as the one at the tail of the bunch went past him, at a range of no more than fifteen feet, Speke shot him out of the saddle, and even before the sombreroed man, arms flailing, hit the ground, Speke was on the move again.

Thick dust was still rising everywhere, picked up and whirled by the gusting wind, but now a strange quiet fell as though the fiercely harassing horsemen had ridden away for some little distance and then had come to a standstill. The wind blew and the dust continued its unceasing movement. In two minds now, Speke went forward hesitantly, his eyes raw and gritty, his filthy clothing sticking to him. This was a Goddamn' mess, bad enough when the posse had got split up, much worse now that both Dryden and Hepburn were dead; especially Hepburn. All those bitter miles he had travelled, all those dangerous places he had been in and all those hard bastards he had faced over more than a quarter of a century, it seemed manifestly unfair for him to finish up in this Godforsaken nowhere, his belly blown out while he had been trying to reassemble a posse that had believed itself to be as good as home.

Girdler, turning from where he had been sheltering behind a dead horse, his left arm hanging, the sleeve copiously bloodied, all but shot at Speke when he came looming out of the dust.

'Jesus! You, Speke...'

'Hepburn's dead,' Speke told him, 'an' Dryden, an' probably Coverdale as well.'

'No. No, the bastards, they got hold of Ed Coverdale. I saw him took. Jesus, this Goddamn' shit that's blowin'!'

'Go on back,' Speke advised. 'Go on

your belly. Keep yelling out to Cady. He's back there about forty yards with George Besant. I'm gonna try to find some of the horses, lead 'em back in. We've got to get the hell out of here.'

'Where's them three bastards we took?'

'With Cady.'

Speke left him. Survivors. Speke himself, Cady, Besant, Girdler. And Coverdale taken. Pardoe? Seen earlier, trying to control his terrified horse, not seen since. Hobbs? Hobbs had called out to Hepburn, telling him about Dryden and Girdler. Speke could not recall seeing him or hearing him after that.

He spent ten minutes attempting to locate more of their horses but could find only one, a roan that had been Coverdale's, and this he led back to where the others were. In his absence Hobbs had reappeared and so had Pardoe, but without his troublesome horse which finally had jerked him off his feet, then bolted. So, counting the three prisoners there were nine men here. Of the posse, Speke, Cady, Besant, Hobbs, the wounded Girdler and Pardoe. But only six horses.

The wind was still taking the white wall of dust across, and the eerie near-silence was still running on. Besant said, 'Mebbe they done pulled out.' Nobody said anything. Besant did not really believe it either. Suddenly Girdler tilted his face on one side.

'Smell it?'

They could now. The dead smell of the dust was now laced with the unmistakable tang of woodsmoke. It was right after that that they heard the man screaming. Cady, as soon as he heard it, began swearing softly and steadily, his dust-caked face taut, his eyes glittering. Hoarsely, Girdler said, 'Jesus Christ A'mighty!'

They sure had got Coverdale and though, because they were loud, the sounds were carrying to them clearly enough, because of the accursed dust nothing could be seen. 'Ain't all that far away,' Hobbs muttered, in itself a suggestion that Ed Coverdale had been brought closer to them, for maximum affect. Besant stood up from his crouching position, and firing and levering fast, sent three lashing, angry shots away.

'Waste of time and bullets,' Cady said.

Besant sank back into his crouch. His sudden firing had drawn no response and it had not put an end to the skin-tingling screaming. Speke looked around at the manacled prisoners. All were huddled together, hats pulled down. Speke thought that, on balance, they had not been worth the trouble, but of course it had not been his posse. His narrowed eyes shifted to look at the dusty, fly-infested lump that was all that remained of the man whose posse it had been, Marshal Charles Hepburn. Speke said what, earlier, he had said to Girdler.

'We've got to get the hell out of here. While the wind's still lifting plenty of dust.'

'Six horses for the nine of us,' Cady said.

'Then we'll need to do some doubling up.'

'Listen,' said Besant.

The screaming had stopped. That quietness did not persist, however, for very soon numerous horses were again on the move, the sounds of them gathering. And suddenly there they were, misted by dust, going quickly by, the riders shooting, lead breathing dangerously over the heads of the now prone possemen and their prisoners.

Besant, Cady and Speke were all firing but there were few real chances. None the less Besant shouted;

'I got one!' Sure enough a man had come tumbling down, flailing, bouncing, rolling, finally to lie still. Speke said, 'It's not one of them.' He pushed the long pistol back in the holster and headed on out. When he made that move, Cady went with him, pistol in hand.

When, soon, they came back, crouching at a half run, they arrived in fresh flurries of dust. Cady, in a hard, dead tone, said,

'It was Ed, what's left of the poor bastard.' Indeed, Coverdale had been shockingly dealt with, cut in a score of places, castrated, his nipples torn from him, then scalped and his eyes burned out with sticks.

Speke said, 'Let's get mounted and make a run for it while we can. There's nothing we can do for Ed, or any of the others.'

'Six animals to carry nine,' Cady repeated, it sounding now like a litany, causing Speke to look hard at him, for Cady's voice was choked with fury, his eyes deeply afire with it in their red-rimmed pits.

'Then we can leave 'em here,' said Speke, of the prisoners.

'We'll leave 'em. We'll sure as hell leave the bastards.' Before Speke realized what was about to take place, Cady had turned on the nearest of them and had unhesitatingly shot the man in the forehead. Speke started to say something even as

Cady's pistol blasted a second time, the next man blown down as Cady shot him in the left eye from close up. By the time this man fell back, the third one, making small, incomprehensible noises in his throat, and while in a squatting posture, was trying to get further away, holding his manacled wrists up in front of his face—as though it was going to make any difference—at the same time losing control of his bladder. When Cady, in his white-hot madness, thrust the barrel of the pistol upwards, under the man's elbows, to plunge it into his mouth, the wretch's head exploded in smoke and blood and mucus, and so the third man died, jerking, and still pissing strongly.

'Get mounted!' Speke yelled, his face draining of blood.

There followed a lot of hauling and shoving, getting the horses ready to head on out, the men swinging up, nobody in charge in the sense that Hepburn had been in charge, but all of a mind to strike out, to head as fast as possible in the direction of Gabriel. Hepburn was indeed dead, his body grossly riven, now no more than a dust-covered lump. So they went heading away, Cady in front followed by Speke, then a bunch, Hobbs, Pardoe, Besant and Girdler.

If they had thought, in these conditions of very poor visibility, that they would get a useful start on those who had been harassing them, they were to be disappointed. Almost at once they knew that the same ravening pursuers were coming, and coming hard. A rifle lashed once, then again. The second shot hit the already wounded, awkwardly riding Girdler, punching him down across the neck of the horse, the man giving a sharp shout as he was hit, Besant calling to the others about it, Cady yelling, 'Keep moving!'

Girdler's horse went veering away to the left, the rider now partially down, one of his boots caught in the stirrup,

Girdler being dragged, the weight of him causing the animal to go galloping in a shallow curve across the stony ground, Girdler taking a savage pummelling, so that Hobbs, glancing back, hoped for that reason and a few others that Girdler was already dead. God alone help him if he was taken alive.

An hour later, having been riding across tough country and finally in among pinnacles of reddish rock, they went angling across a grainy fan of an ancient lava-flow, seeking to get themselves among other, larger, time-ravaged rocks and some small canyons, the broken beginnings of the High Torres. They came to a ragged halt, looking back as they had looked back scores of times. Far behind them now, between dun-coloured earth and brassy sky, was spread the long, yellowish bar that was the wind-blown dust, and under which lay numerous men, some good, some manifestly bad, together with several horses. Breathing hard, all looking haggard, surprisingly it was the complainer, Pardoe, who said, 'We sure did put some distance on 'em.'

Hobbs hawked and spat noisily. 'Mebbe they stopped to fry Girdler.'

They might well have put some distance on those who had been coming after them, but it had sure cost their horses, all blowing, heads hanging, not fit to make another run like that one for a while.

Speke said, nodding, 'We'd do well to get up among the rocks, yonder, well out of sight, to spell the animals.'

'Ondero River's on'y eight, ten mile,' Hobbs reminded them.

Cady asked: 'That hang-dog mule you're on, has he got as much as a mile left in him?'

Hobbs made no response, knowing that Cady was reinforcing what Speke had been saying, and knowing too, no doubt, that his own anxiety to be on the move was being driven by fear alone; but he did not want to have that exposed. Poor old Ed

Coverdale. *The bastards.*

This posse had come out, come a hell of a long way, mainly on information that had come Hepburn's way two or three weeks back, of four men, long wanted on counts of robbery and rape—one of those of a child of twelve—being holed up in a place south-west of Gabriel. By some thoughtful planning, Hepburn had taken them—well, three out of the four—but it had turned out to be too easy. The men he had got hold of had been there waiting to be joined by others, getting ready, so Hepburn had belatedly come to believe, to move cattle from spreads up around Gabriel right down to the border. Well, belated theories had been all very well. Behind what was left of Hepburn's posse lay those who had died the most horrifying of deaths.

When they all dismounted in the place that, finally, they chose, well enough hidden they believed, it was almost sundown. They risked no fire. Pardoe, with a rifle, went trudging back to a spot from which he could get a view of the approaches, at least while the light lasted. They had canteens but water was low; but reasonably early tomorrow they would get to the Ondero where there would be ample water, even in this dry season, for both men and animals.

Hobbs and Besant stretched out on their bedrolls. Speke and Cady sat propped against a smooth boulder.

'I have to ask myself,' said Cady, 'what the hell I'm doing here and in these straits. You remember my dad, the preacher?'

'I remember him,' Speke said. The only part of the Reverend Wilmot Cady that seemed to have come through to his handsome son was the quiet, almost musical tone of voice; and then Speke was ruminative about whether or not the occasional, blazing episodes of fury might therefore have been the gift of the sly-eyed, part-Cheyenne woman, Jeb Cady's mother. Speke then had to bring out what was on his mind. 'We could have left them there, alive, all three.'

'I can see it's been damn' well eating at you,' Cady said. He was no longer showing evidence of the anger that had consumed him when he had pistolled the three manacled men, and all before you could spit, maddened, it had seemed, first by Hepburn's ugly death, then because of what had been done to Ed Coverdale.

'Kin of yours, was he, Coverdale? If he was I must've missed it.'

'No.'

Speke had killed men but never in that manner. He had never been able to work Cady out. In a corner like the one they had been in, and were not out of yet come to that, there would be no one that he would rather have with him; but what had occurred today, whatever the circumstances, had sickened Speke. Now he wanted shut of it all; he wanted to break free, get some time to himself, maybe, if he could contrive it, go visit Montressor, where those two Rawlins sisters happened to live.

A day and a half later the subdued, exhausted survivors of a posse that had gone out in strength and good heart had come bobbing silently back into Gabriel.

THREE

In their own room, Harriet now left in hers to sleep with greater peace of mind than she had known in some weeks, Meg Rawlins and Speke had their own affairs to talk about. Sabina had not been anywhere in their plans but now, it seemed, it was.

'I don't fancy the sound of any of this,' Meg said. She was now in her nightdress and blue robe and her hair was loose and fallen about her shoulders. Seated at a much scratched and chipped dresser she was looking at Speke's reflection in the mirror. He had put his valise on the lower end of the bed and opened it, and from it had taken a thickly shelled belt, holster and .44 Smith and Wesson, a lovingly kept weapon with a much-fingered handle; a large pistol, well suited to Speke's big hand. On the floor at the end of the bed, in its scabbard, lay his Winchester repeater.

Unfailingly, Meg got a strange hollow feeling in her stomach whenever she saw him critically examining either of the weapons, making the most meticulous of checks, the oiled mechanisms clicking thickly as he tested them, each of the sounds brutally familiar to her, even after all this time; sounds, indeed, that she could never hear without repressing this small tremor of distaste.

How completely absorbed he was when he was doing this. How stolidly stern he looked, with his thick, dark brows and his teak-like face and fierce black moustaches, a large and powerful man whose reputation often travelled with him, or all too frequently preceded him. John Hammond Speke, a pistolman. Yet in all of their time together, only on one occasion had she actually seen him shooting. That had been years ago at a place called South

Camp, for the most part, at that time, no more than a string of nondescript soddies strewn along a tributary of the LeBrun River, and a place where she and Speke had had to stop because one of the horses had thrown a shoe; and the shooting had not been at a man, but *men*. Two of them, there had been, foul and unkempt, dressed in leather leggings and bulky coats of animal fur, half drunk, workless itinerants, sufficiently fired up on sour whiskey not to pay sufficient attention to the tall, quiet man.

It had been Meg herself who had quickly taken their eye as she waited near one of the soddies while Speke was away bargaining with a man who had said he could do the forging. They had got her backed up against the soddy and one even had his dirt-caked hand up her skirts when Speke had come pacing back and called to them.

One had an old Colt shoved down inside the broad belt that was holding his coat closed, the other a long, heavy Sharps that he had leaned against the wall of the soddy in order to have both hands free for the woman. What they had seen when they had stepped away from her had been the big, hard-looking man with his brown, knee-length coat slung back on one side to expose the curved handle of a pistol, but because they had been half drunk, filled with the false boldness that goes with that condition, again failed to accord this somewhat frightening man due respect.

The one carrying the Colt had tugged the weapon from his belt and in a thunderclap of sound and a start of smoke that had come bursting around Speke, had been bashed backwards, the smack of the lead heard clearly by the woman who was only a couple of yards from the man who had been hit. The second man had got hold of the heavy Sharps, the kind of weapon that could put a hole like a railroad tunnel in man or beast, and had begun turning with it, bringing it up, when Speke had come pacing forward, his face like some terrible demon emerging from the Pit, blasting the .44, jolting the man with the Sharps, turning him, punching him again and again.

When the sudden, frightening sounds had ceased, though smoke had still been hanging around and the sharp tang of spent powder had been on the air, people had slowly come out of the soddies, pale women like hesitant troglodytes with lank hair, sunk-eyed children, men with beaten eyes, all come to stare at the dead men who, in their fur coats, had resembled a pair of shot animals.

Speke, his pistol put away, had looked around and asked the general question: 'Know these two?'

Heads had been shaken. 'They sure don't belong in these parts, mister.'

'They do now,' Speke had said.

Speke was clicking his fingers in front of her face as he bent forward, studying it in the mirror. She gave a small shake of her head and what was almost a laugh.

He asked, 'Where were you?'

After a moment's pause, she said, 'South Camp.'

Speke straightened. 'That was long ago, Megs.'

'Yes.' But for her it was never really long ago. It was simply that she had not mentioned the name of the place in a long while. But now she said, 'You're going on to Sabina?'

'The way she is, would you have me do otherwise?'

'I guess not.' Then, 'Oh, God, I don't know, John. He's such a prideful man. He'll want her to go back. No, he'll *expect* her to go back. But she can't, she mustn't.'

'Then he still owes her what's hers and a lot more besides. If I don't carry that message to Jeb, then nobody else is about to.'

'Maybe she should hire an attorney from

somewhere. We could—'

'And have this drag out for a year? More? Then there's the matter of cost. If I go talk with him and I get nowhere, then maybe she can go to an attorney. At least she'd have gotten an answer that an attorney could start to work on.'

'John, I've said I don't like the sounds of it at all, no matter how long you've known Jeb Cady.' But she could recognize the deep, if slow-moving anger in him, no doubt remembering, as she was, the awful battering to Harriet's body. What he said then confirmed that.

'I can't abide the sight of what he did to her, Megs, no more than you can. I'll not let that matter lie, say nothing.'

Their eyes met in the mirror before he turned away. Meg's eyes went on looking at the speckled glass. The signs of ageing were indeed before her but she did not tell him what was in her mind: *God, I'm almost in middle age. And what's this year going to bring us? More ill luck? More risks?* More moving from place to place, a peacekeeper's job here, another there. Payment made for a skilled pistolman. Speke was getting older, too, and soon his reflexes must suffer, his renowned physical toughness soften. No one could go on forever. So, then what? They had few savings. He had earned well but there had been times when they had lived well, too. And there was an increasing fear, for her, that sooner or later, whenever Speke's powers were widely known to be in decline, that at least one of those who would not have dared face him in his prime, would arrive to settle some old score.

He said, 'You want to take one more look at Harriet?'

Deliberately she said, 'You go.' He was still fully dressed. Even so, it was as though she was overtly testing him, even daring him to say something. Yet what was it that she was expecting? Maybe there *was* nothing. Maybe it was nothing more than a demon that had formed and grown in her own mind because she was as old as she was, and Harriet was seven years younger; and looking it, even in her present abused condition.

'As you wish.' Flat, non-committal, his tone of voice. Harriet had wanted her sister to lock her door and take charge of the key, such was her unsettlement of mind. Now Meg handed it to Speke. He went out. After only a few minutes he reappeared and handed her the key back. 'Sleeping soundly. She hasn't moved.' Then, 'I'm going on down to that livery, take a look at 'em. If the mercantile's still open, maybe I'll pick up a few things I'll need for the journey.'

'What time will you leave for Sabina?'

'Early.'

She began brushing her hair. Not looking at him, she said, 'Don't be too long.'

Schaeffer's livery and corral was two blocks down and in a sidestreet. Speke visited it and spoke to the man there, saying he would come by tomorrow, probably around sunup, for the black horse. 'Be gone a few days. See you take damn' good care of that bay.' He went out, the liveryman's eyes following him speculatively.

Speke was back on the main street pacing along one of the boardwalks. Not many townsfolk were to be seen now, though a couple of the saloons were still noisy with laughter and jangly music. Then he remembered that he ought to call in at the mercantile which happened to be on the opposite side of the street, its lamps still burning.

About to cross over, he paused. Right alongside the mercantile was the Harper House Hotel, and two men were in the act of dismounting at the tie-rail there. Speke's highly developed sixth sense teased the hairs at the nape of his neck. There was something about these men. They were not range riders—at least, they were not dressed as such—nor, plainly, were they homesteaders. No, there was a very different look to these two, and it was not only that they were in possession of good horseflesh and what seemed to be, at this distance and in this light, well-kept equipment.

Both were wearing long, buff dusters and wide-brimmed hats with medium crowns. Their saddles and other gear seemed to be in excellent condition. They tied their horses and went up on the boardwalk and inside the Harper House. Marshals? That was only Speke's second thought, though, and even then he was trying to rationalize the first thing that had come into his mind after what Harriet had said.

Instead of heading across to the mercantile, Speke continued on to the Alonquin, and once there, he waited in the hotel's doorway, but standing back a little, away from the spread of the outside lamplight. He glanced around. The clerk was not in his booth so was probably sitting in the box-like room at the back of it. Almost ten minutes elapsed before the two riders came out of the Harper House and, leaving their mounts where they had tied them, came angling across the main street, obviously heading for the Alonquin.

Speke eased his long body back inside. Not far from the foot of the stairs was a closed door leading to an office. On the toes of his boots he crossed the poorly lit lobby, tried the door handle, eased the door open and went inside the darkened, unoccupied room. He did not close the door behind him but held it open a matter of two or three inches so that the stairway and the clerk's booth could both be seen.

He heard their boots first, then there they were, one a man nearly as tall as Speke himself, with broad hands and a broken nose, the other not as tall, round of face, with long, reddish sideburns. The taller one rapped on the counter of the booth and the clerk came bobbing into view.

Speke, examining the visitors as closely as he could, now wished that he had paused to buckle on the pistol before coming out. It had been an act of carelessness for which he was silently castigating himself. It was not long before his worst apprehensions were confirmed.

The tall man said, 'We're makin' enquiries all over fer a missin' woman by the name o' Cady. Mrs Harriet Cady.'

The clerk, eyeglasses glinting, stood staring at them, evidently not caring much for the looks of them, for he seemed uncomfortable. 'We've got more than a dozen folks in the house,' he said.

The gingery man said, 'An' all their names'll be in the register, so let's take us a look.' If the clerk had been about to protest, even resist, he changed his mind when the other one said,

'Now. We come a long way an' we ain't got all night.'

The clerk dragged the heavy book to him, opened it and looked, then glanced up. 'No, nobody by the name of Cady.'

The gingery man would not leave it

at that, but reached across and took possession of the register, turning it around on the counter. Both men looked at it, the bigger one running a finger down the names. Speke waited. They would find no entry for Cady. Among others, they would find a Mr and Mrs Speke (though that was an untruth) and a Miss H. Rawlins, which was Harriet's maiden name. Driven by her fears of being sought, it had been something she had asked for before Speke had gone out to book the rooms.

The shorter man, who was no longer making much of an effort to study the register, was instead staring at the clerk. 'Kinda small, dark-haired woman, real good lookin'. Wears a brown cloak with a hood.'

If the clerk made the connection right off he did not give any indication of it; but the tall man said, 'You think about it real careful, mister.' The fact that he had discovered no *Mrs Cady* seemed to have left him unconvinced. The clerk licked his lips, then offered, tentatively,

'There was a sick lady. I recall she had on a brown cloak.' Still *sick* in the clerk's mind, anyway.

'Sick lady?'

'She didn't come in on her own. She was, uh, brought in.'

Again the tall man looked at the register. 'Which one?'

Partly screwing his head around so that he could see, the clerk said, 'There. Number eleven. Miss Rawlins. It was Mr and Mrs Speke that brought her in.'

The tall man stood scraping thick fingers at his jaw, not quite decided, but then he said, 'We'd best have us a word, jes' to be sure.'

'I can't allow that,' the clerk said with unexpected decisiveness. After all, the house did have rules and he had already stood by and watched them break one of those by looking in the register. But like Mr Speke, earlier, they had not struck him as men that it would be wise to argue with too stubbornly on points of principle.

'One way or the other, mister, we're gonna have us a word with this here Miss Rawlins.'

Neither of them heard Speke come out of the darkened office but the clerk sure saw him, and the man's eyes seemed to fill his eyeglasses.

'That won't be necessary,' Speke said.

They did not turn in a real hurry for by no means were they naturally nervous men. They merely looked, then turned fully.

'Who the hell are *you?*' the gingery one asked.

'John Speke.'

If it meant something, they did not say so, nor did their dead faces alter one whit.

The taller one said, 'He says yuh brought a woman here.'

Speke said: 'No, I brought two women here, my wife and her sister, Miss Rawlins. Right now they're both in bed asleep and nobody is about to disturb either of them for any reason.' Unhurriedly the two at the booth now separated until they were three feet apart and were standing well clear of the booth. The clerk had gradually gone backing away, his wide eyes shuttling from Speke to the two men in the long dusters and back again. 'You the law from somewhere or other?' Speke inquired.

'Nope. We work for Mr Cady, in Sabina County. His wife, she's gone missin', so we're out askin' all over.'

'There's some law here in Denton,' Speke said. 'A telegram to the sheriff would've got the same questions asked, and a damn' sight faster.'

'How Mr Cady wants it done is his Goddamn' business,' the ginger man said sharply, and added, 'In Sabina he's the town marshal, an' a lot more besides.'

'I know that,' said Speke.

'What?'

'Unless I miss my guess, he'd be Jeb Cady,' Speke said.

'John...Speke,' the tall man said. Now it

had started coming to him, not necessarily from anything that he had learned from Cady, much more likely through other word that, over time, had come to him on the wind, wherever he had been. Their eyes had already slid to Speke's middle before coming back to his unwavering eyes. No pistol. Well, no pistol in plain view. Maybe they were trying to work out where it could be, for now it would be firmly planted in both their minds that there would *be* one. He was a known pistolman. It was what he did. They were not afraid of him, however, that was plain enough, which was not to say that they were not naturally wary of him.

The tall one, who seemed to be much the more fly of the two, said, 'She's Mrs Cady, ain't she? The woman yuh brought in, sick?'

'If she is, then it still makes no difference. All that Jeb Cady's going to get from Denton is a message from me. The message is this: 'I'm on my way to

Sabina. There are things that have to be talked about, and they're all strictly between me and him.' That's all. That message. There's nothing else for you to get, here.'

The ginger one seemed to be about to jump in and say something but the other extended a hand slightly to deter him.

'That's been made plain enough, Mr Speke. Now we know where we stand. That's the message that'll be took.'

'Then I'm obliged to you, Mr...'

'Griffin. Jack Griffin. An' this here's Charlie Redruth.'

Speke nodded. They walked out of the lobby of the Alonquin and onto the boardwalk. Speke stood listening as the sounds of their clumping boots diminished, then he looked at the clerk.

'I'll bid you goodnight.' He went on up the stairs but his mind was much disturbed. They had gone, just like that. It had been too easy. Now he wondered if he dare leave the two women in Denton while he went on to meet Cady; yet Harriet was in no fit state to travel anywhere, even to get her further away.

FOUR

Speke turned the lamp up, but not too brightly. The bedclothes whispered as Meg sat up, her hair in disarray She had been lying there waiting for him; but now one look was enough.

'John, what's wrong?'

'They're here,' Speke said. 'Two of 'em. They were at the Harper House and they were downstairs, asking, but they've gone now.'

'They saw you?' She had flung back the covers and was getting out of bed, reaching to the foot of it for her robe.

'Yes, I've talked with 'em some. I chose to do that. Gave 'em a message for Jeb.'

'Will they take it? I mean, will they just leave?'

'I don't know, Megs. They've left the

Alonquin, that's all I can say.' She was tying the robe; pulling it in emphasized her slimness. Speke was at the window now, fingering aside the brown shade, looking down at a wedge of the main street. 'Quiet. Not much doing.' But it was probable that at the best of times there was not a whole lot doing in Denton. 'One thing,' he said, 'if they're still in town tomorrow, they'll stand out.'

'You'll not be leaving though, 'til you're sure?'

'I'd say not.' Now he glanced around at her. 'Harriet sure was right about this, Megs, that Jeb would likely send people looking.'

'But not to harm her, surely?'

'To take her back to Sabina. Make sure of getting it done. That's all to do with his pride of course. Jeb doesn't cotton to failure, never did. He would sure be concerned that other people, when they got to hear of it, would see this as a failure. *His* failure, therefore a weakness.

He'd want to have things put back the way they were, on his terms.'

'Surely some in Sabina must have got to know what was going on between him and Harriet. I mean, there must have been times when she couldn't go out in public, maybe for weeks on end.'

Speke favoured her with a somewhat sour smile. 'If Jeb has the power that Harriet says he's got, and you were only Joe Townsman, would you want to get mixed up in his personal affairs, or would you just mind your own business? Anyway, you've got to get a look at the pair of wolves who were down in the lobby to understand how things really are in Sabina. I wouldn't take either of 'em cheaply.'

Clearly Meg was worried anew about her sister's predicament. 'We should go take a look at her. I'll get the key. Will you do it?'

'Yes.' But for the moment, having come away from the window, he had lifted his valise onto a chair. She knew that the pistol would be coming out again.

At that same time, however, there came a light tapping on the door. Meg stiffened. Speke called, 'Who is it?'

The clerk's rather pipey voice said, 'It's me, Mr Speke...the hotel clerk. There's a message been left.'

Speke stepped to the door and opened it. Sure enough, there was the clerk, his eyes swollen behind his eyeglasses and there was sweat shining on his face. Something had sure put the fear of Old Nick into him and, upon seeing his condition, Speke felt a stab of unease.

'What's the message?' asked Speke.

'It's this,' the gingery Redruth said, stepping into view, pistol now extended, close to the clerk's neck. 'We come to Denton lookin' fer Mrs Cady. Now we know she's here, an' we sure ain't leavin' without her. Her door's locked. Where's the key?'

Speke gauged his own chances of getting this door slammed and diving for the .44

in the open valise but soon assessed them as next to nothing. The risk to Meg would be too great and, for another thing, the clerk would be as good as dead. Behind him, Meg was absolutely still. While not even turning his face to her, Speke said, 'This man is Charlie Redruth and he's one of Jeb Cady's employees.'

'An' I'm another one,' Griffin said, and the tall man came walking along the hall, a pistol in his hand also, but hanging by his side. Both men were still in their long, buff-coloured dusters and wearing their hats. 'An' what Redruth says is right. We're gonna take Mrs Cady home.'

Meg said, 'She's sleeping.'

'Anybody that's asleep can soon be woke up,' Redruth said, 'so go do it.'

'She's not well enough to go anywhere,' said Meg, 'not tonight.'

'Lady,' said Redruth, 'it's been one hell of a long day an' I ain't gonna stand here arguin' the toss about this. Mrs Cady's here. We want her. Go git her.'

Speke said, 'Best do as he wants. Get the key, Megs.'

Redruth looked squarely at Speke. 'Fer the pistolman we've heard yuh was, Speke, yuh don't carry one, reg'lar.'

'I do when I have to,' Speke said. But it was a truth that was already tearing at him and he had the feeling that Redruth knew it very well.

To Meg, Redruth said again, 'Go in there now an' git her, lady, an' don't take all night about it.' To make that possible he went backing off to the opposite side of the hall, pulling the sweating clerk along with him. Griffin, too, had now retreated a few paces so that he could get a view all along the hall and down onto the stair-landing as well. They had not expected to run up against anybody like Speke, and for all they knew he might have associates in this town. Later, maybe, they would try to work out how Speke himself had got into this at all.

Meg walked out of their room and went

into Harriet's next door, and presently those in the hallway—and Speke, too, who had stepped clear of the doorway—could hear the low voices of the women. Several minutes went by until finally Redruth said, 'What the hell's keepin' 'em?'

'My wife will be helping her sister to get dressed,' said Speke evenly. Then he said, 'You remember this, Redruth, you too, Griffin: you've been told this woman is ill. She's not fit to travel. She's certainly not fit to go ten yards on horseback. If anything bad should happen to her while you've got her, it's Jeb Cady you'll have to answer to, not me. And by God, if that comes to pass, the entire country won't be big enough for you to hide in.'

It did have some sort of effect, but in a certain defence, Griffin said, 'She ain't gonna be on a horse.'

That must mean that they had got hold of some sort of vehicle, and one of them would have to drive it. And it meant they were not going to be able to travel as quickly as they would have done, all on horses.

There was a rustling sound, of skirts, and Harriet came out of her room, but being helped by Meg. Harriet was wearing her brown, hooded cloak. She was moving slowly, her head down. Griffin said, 'Evenin' Mrs Cady.'

Looking up, she said, 'Oh, it's you...'

Redruth was giving Harriet what was plainly a hungry stare. This man must often have looked at her in that way, thought Speke, but had been constrained, as he would be now, to keep a certain distance from her. Only a hopeless lunatic would go as far as putting a hand on Jeb Cady's woman. So in that respect, Speke considered, Harriet would travel in safety.

Harriet's eyes lingered on Speke. 'I'm sorry, John, for...getting you *involved*.'

'We came of our own accord,' Speke said.

Harriet nodded slightly. Then, 'We'll maybe...work something out, me and Jeb.

We'll see...' Probably she did not believe it any more than he did; or Meg.

Meg, even dressed as she was in her night attire, would have gone downstairs with Harriet, but at once Griffin shook his head. 'No need fer that, Mrs Speke. From here on we'll take charge of Mrs Cady.' To Speke he said, 'You stay up here too, Speke, an' try settin' on your hands. If there's any trouble blows up, there's a risk this here lady could git hurt. You wouldn't want to see that any more'n Mr Cady would.'

'I understand that,' said Speke. 'Tell Cady I'm still coming to talk with him.'

Meg glanced at Speke. After this new development she had not quite expected that. But Speke was staring only at Cady's men as they began helping Harriet down the stairs, or rather Griffin did, while Charlie Redruth, one hand bunching the clerk's shirt, went backing down, still watching Speke carefully as though he was some kind of highly poisonous spider.

Slowly, in that fashion, they all passed from Speke's view.

Choking back a sob, Meg came to Speke, and with one arm he held her to him, but he said, 'C'mon, Megs. Inside.'

And as soon as they were in the room he released her and went very fast to the open valise and lifted the Smith and Wesson out.

'John...for God's sake... You can't...'

'Take it easy Megs.' It was said softly, kindly.

Pausing in the doorway to look towards the stairs, making sure that Charlie Redruth had not come back for a second look, he then went on the toes of his boots along the hall, but in the opposite direction. There was a branch of the hall that led off at right angles, and sure enough, as Speke had fervently hoped there would be, a flight of narrow back stairs. Speke, though making efforts to keep noises muffled, went down these three at a time. He did not want to use the pistol he was now carrying, but he was sure not going anywhere else tonight without it, even though he had not paused to buckle on the shellbelt. Paramount, though, was Harriet's safety, and that no doubt was what Griffin and Redruth were banking on, too. Harriet was their trump card.

Between finding the back stairs and quietly letting himself out into the back yard of the Alonquin, Speke had encountered no-one. There was not much light to go by out here. He went picking his way along an alley at the side of the hotel, one which seemed to have acquired more than its share of junk. Speke bumped a shin against something unyielding and swore softly. More circumspectly he approached the paint-peeling corner of the Alonquin.

Once there, Speke stopped to take a cautious look onto the street and saw at once that he was favoured in two respects. First, so far there was no sign of the slow-moving Harriet and the two men from Sabina; second, their horses were at the Alonquin tie-rail and there, also, standing between the light shafts of a covered buggy, was a single, roan horse, so that the back of the buggy was only a few feet from where Speke was. He could now hear voices and drew back slightly.

By the glow of the lantern above the door of the Alonquin, Griffin was coming into view holding Harriet by one arm, supporting her in her painful-looking progress. As soon as they were out, Redruth appeared, and as he did, he was in the act of putting his pistol away.

Speke eased back even further as Redruth unhitched one of the saddle-horses and brought it around to be tied to the back of the buggy, this obviously the horse belonging to the man who was to do the driving. While Redruth was occupied with that task, Speke was so close to him that he could almost have reached out and touched him, so Speke thought it was the best chance he was ever going to get, Redruth with his back to him, Griffin helping Harriet along the boardwalk towards the buggy.

Speke came out from the sheltering corner of the building and in one long stride stepped behind Redruth and brought the barrel of the pistol down in a glittering arc to thump solidly onto the man's hat, then a second savage blow that made a heavy clunking sound and drove Redruth to his knees, to fall against a rear wheel of the buggy.

By that time, however, Speke was already on his way towards Griffin. Harriet, to her credit, in the jumbled seconds during which Redruth was struck down and the big figure of Speke was almost across to them, leaned as heavily as she could against the tall man so that his instinct was to save her from falling down. But that instinct did not endure for longer than a few heartbeats, Griffin managing to disengage himself to sweep aside his now loose duster to reach for his pistol. Harriet was on her hands and knees on the boardwalk trying to crawl away while Speke, having closed in, but not wanting to shoot, struck out with his left fist, catching Griffin on the left cheekbone, sending him staggering away.

Speke thrust the pistol down inside his belt and followed up fast. Griffin's hat had gone spinning away and the long duster, flapping around him, was proving a hindrance as he attempted to pull the pistol free. But Speke now closed with the man, grasping him, wrestling him back along the boardwalk, both of them bumping hard against the front wall of the Alonquin.

Harriet, her legs drawn up under her, was sitting on the boardwalk several yards away, also leaning against the Alonquin, while the man Speke had so savagely pistol-whipped, Redruth, was on his knees, his body arched over, his forehead pressing on the street as though he was intent on biting at the dirt; and he had one shoulder lodged against a wheel of the buggy. Obviously Redruth did not know where the hell he was.

Griffin, as Speke had believed from the start, was not going to be any pushover. Now that initial surprise and confusion were behind him he had begun fighting back strongly. But Speke had accumulated a fund of resentment against Jeb Cady and therefore against those who had come here in his name. The sight of the hurts to Harriet's body was still vivid in his mind and it was that which was now fuelling his energy in the fight with Jack Griffin.

Well matched for weight and height, both were now launching hard blows. The heavy pistol that Speke had shoved down in his belt soon became dislodged and fell clattering to the boardwalk. Lurching and punching they went out onto the street itself, not a great deal of noise to their fighting, so drawing no onlookers, even though saloons further along the street still had customers.

While Speke and Griffin fought, Redruth was slowly gathering his wits. He put one hand on the wheel of the buggy, then grasped a spoke and began hauling himself upright. Awareness was coming back to him, but slowly, and once or twice he was compelled to pause in his efforts to stand, his head sinking down. Yet, trying to blink away lights that were passing across his vision, Redruth did manage to get himself upright, though leaning against the buggy for support. As his vision gradually cleared he could discern in the spread of light from the Alonquin's lantern, Harriet Cady. She was sitting on the boardwalk huddled against the dusty boards of the hotel, her legs drawn up under her. Scuffling and grunting noises a little way off, then a glimpse of figures against the glow of a distant saloon, revealed to him where Griffin was. And Speke.

His head still slightly swimming, Redruth started along the boardwalk in the direction of the fighting men, one of his hands fumbling down for the butt of the pistol beneath the flapping duster. He had progressed beyond the doorway of the Alonquin, intent on giving help to Griffin, when Meg's voice said, 'No further than that, Mr Redruth.' Mouth falling open, blinking, the ginger-headed man turned to look at her.

Meg, in her light, tied robe, was standing in the doorway of the Alonquin. She was holding Speke's Winchester. Slowly Redruth moved his open duster back. The dirty-handled pistol was hanging against his right leg. Meg's pulses were throbbing, her mouth feeling sour, a taste there like vomit. The problem for Redruth, given away by the rapid blinking of his eyes, was that his sight was still furry and therefore the small woman with the rifle was not as distinct as she ought to have been; but he was still weighing the probability of her actually firing the rifle if he did manage to clear his pistol away quickly.

As though tracking all of these thoughts, Meg now lifted the Winchester so that the butt-plate was against her thin shoulder, and she leaned back in the door-corner the better to steady herself. Very slowly now, Redruth brought his hand away from near the handle of the pistol and allowed the duster to slip down again, covering the weapon.

'Pistolman's whore!'

'I'd hoped you'd let me prove to you that I'd kill for him, Mr Redruth.' Without turning her head, her eyes fixedly on Redruth, Meg called softly, 'Harriet?'

'I hear you. I'm...all right.'

Still Speke and Griffin fought. Then Griffin swung the kind of predictable, roundhouse punch that wiped through empty air, missing its target, and that was what Speke had been hoping for, for as Griffin swung across him, slightly unbalanced, Speke lashed out and up with a boot that went crashing into the other man's groin. Griffin screamed and doubled over, and Speke, taking his time about it, steadied and kicked the other man in the face. The tall man was jolted upwards, arms splaying as Speke moved in fast on an open target and punched him hard in the throat, and Griffin went down, writhing and choking. Speke crossed to him and pulled the pistol away and flung it into the darkness, then turned and walked back to where Redruth stood.

When he saw the three of them, Meg propped and holding the rifle, Harriet sitting against the wall of the Alonquin, Speke said to Redruth, 'Get that buggy back to wherever you hired it. You won't be needing it. Then go get that long piece of shit back there across his horse and leave here, the pair of you. Deliver my message to Jeb Cady. By God, mister, don't you still be in this town when the sky gets light. One more thing: after tomorrow, nobody need bother coming to Denton looking for Mrs Cady. She won't be here.'

That was a lie but it might provide both of the women with some peace of mind, some safety, for a short while at least. Long enough, so Speke hoped.

FIVE

Reddish scores on Speke's face were shiny
with salve as were the cut knuckles of his
big hands. In the early morning he had
just come in from prowling the streets of
Denton and visiting its liveries and corrals.
During those investigations he had found
the one from which the buggy had been
hired. The vehicle had been returned. Of
the two men from Sabina he had been
able to find no trace. A swamper outside
one of the saloons had been able to say
that a ginger-headed man of Redruth's
description had come in very late on the
previous night to buy whiskey.

'So they've gone,' Harriet said. Very
pale, with dark rings below her eyes, she
was dressed in a robe over her nightdress,
and sitting in a chair, watching, as her

sister made up the bed again.

'I found not hide nor hair,' Speke said.

'I hope it means the same thing,' said Meg.

Speke asked, 'You want me to leave the rifle?'

Meg looked up from arranging pillows. 'No.'

It was Harriet, however, who asked Meg, 'Would you have shot him?'

Meg carried on smoothing a pillow, then said, 'Yes.' She gave something like a sigh as she straightened up. 'If you'd asked me the same question this time yesterday, I would have said *never*. But for the first time in my life I came close to understanding how it is that people can kill. But I doubt I could do it again, get that close.'

Speke said, 'I've seen the likes of Charlie Redruth before. He'd not back down easily. He'd never have believed that he'd back down to a woman. You convinced him, or he'd have tried for the pistol. So there was something that told him that you'd do it if you had to.'

Harriet's big, sad eyes were still fixed on Meg. Witnessing it all she had now come to realize that Charlie Redruth had indeed been only a heartbeat from death, and not for the first time did she ponder over the strong bond between her sister and this hard, sometimes frightening, always uncompromising man.

Meg said, 'Afterwards, I felt sick.'

'That's because *you* know you would have done it,' said Speke. Then, 'I've paid up for these rooms for a week and paid the livery for the bay. Here.' He handed Meg a thick fold of bills.

'John, there's a lot here.'

'I've kept enough back to see me through.'

She stared at him, fearing now that he really meant that he wanted her to be holding nearly all their money in case something went badly wrong. Now he was ready to go. He had on black pants and boots, a blue shirt with a black string tie and a thigh-length coat. In one hand he was holding a wide-brimmed, somewhat ill-used black hat. Around his still lean middle was a wide, studded leather belt, and angled down to the right, a full shellbelt, the new loads gleaming, and thonged to his right thigh a worn holster, the handle of the Smith and Wesson curving out of it. He stooped and picked up the scabbarded Winchester.

'You've been to the mercantile?' she asked.

'Yes. The black's ready, tied out front. There's no use to delay.'

'John, for God's sake be careful...'

'Don't worry yourself Megs. I know Jeb, he knows me.'

Meg stretched up and kissed his leathery face. Harriet, her cheeks wet, had him stoop to receive her kiss.

He left them.

The sun had fired far distant peaks with

the last of its rays before Speke came into the town of Rachman, the town where Harriet had taken the stage for Denton. By the time Speke had visited a livery where he left the black to be fed and watered and had toted what little stuff he had brought with him, in saddlebags, to an hotel, had found a barber, then, freshly shaved, taken a bath and a meal, the full evening had come down.

After he had eaten he went for a prowl around the town, looking at any horses at the tie-rails—as he had run his eye over horses that were on view at the livery he had chosen—and had also glanced inside a couple of saloons. Though of course he could not be certain of it, it did seem that neither Griffin nor Redruth, if indeed they had been in the place, were anywhere around Rachman. On the way here, on the trail between Denton and this town, he had travelled steadily but with some caution, even though he had noticed few places where Cady's men might have lain in wait for him. Indeed he had by no means discounted the possibility that Redruth in particular might not be beyond taking a shot at him if the opportunity came. Then again, maybe the wiser counsels of the battered Jack Griffin would prevail; or maybe neither were in fit shape even to contemplate it.

Now, lying on the bed in his poky hotel room, his boots and coat off but otherwise fully dressed, Speke wondered again about the possibility that the two he had run up against would really do anything on their own initiative, no matter how aggrieved they felt. Possibly their having failed to fetch Harriet away and the reach of Jeb Cady's authority would be strong enough to restrain them.

So he thought about Meg and about Harriet, and now worried that he had not chosen to wait, taken the option, perhaps, in a day or two, of Harriet's being able to be sent on, by stage, with Meg, to say, Lowndes Crossing, or even further. Just to be sure. Now that he had not only been seen to have helped her but had run up against Cady's two searchers, he had to consider the possibility that Cady's reaction might well be extreme when he got to hear about it.

Meg and Harriet. There had been times in the past, when Harriet's name had come up, that Meg had seemed to regard him oddly, as though she was trying to see right into his mind. That had been the case in the last moments before he had left them, Harriet, in her gratitude, wanting to kiss him. Speke had never been able to deny the thought that Harriet, from her much younger days, had exuded a certain sensuality that no man, if he were to be truthful, might ignore altogether. Thus could Speke begin to understand the powerful attraction Harriet had had for Cady as soon as he had set eyes on her; and that made it all the more difficult to understand how that same man could have even contemplated striking her. Speke drew in a deep breath and wished himself further along on the journey to Sabina.

Because he was now anxious to get this business over and done with, he was pressing on from Rachman towards Sabina with a little more urgency than he had on the Denton to Rachman leg. But it was not only a desire to talk with Jeb Cady, to put Harriet's argument for her and to boldly declare himself and Meg as witnesses to the treatment that Harriet had received, but also a wish to get back to Meg as soon as he could so that the two of them could resume their interrupted journey; for by that time, Meg's sister might be sufficiently recovered in health and spirit to go her own way, with, so Speke hoped, her due recompense from Cady in hand. If that man indeed placed a high value on his standing within the Sabina community, then Speke believed that he was now heading towards him carrying some powerful cards.

He was following the trail through some dry, broken country now, high, rock-jutting ground on either hand, hardy brush clinging to the rough slopes, the ridges green with wind-warped pines. The black was going easily though, and Speke himself was today feeling less sore and stiff from his hard encounter with Griffin, and his abrasions were healing. Hard men, those, but given a hard message to go with the other that he had told them they must carry to Cady. By now, too, the story from the clerk at the Alonquin would have swept through the town. *John Speke, he did that to those men, right here in Denton.* If nothing else, it would likely provide Meg with some quite wary but courteous treatment. And a liveryman would have another snippet to be passed around: Speke would be gone but a few days.

Speke hauled back on the reins, fetching the black to a halt and, even as the horse stopped, head tossing, Speke was getting out of the saddle fast, clawing a hand back to unscabbard the rifle as he did so.

His eye had caught the bright wink of sun on metal, ahead and above, and as through filmy dust he now dragged at the black's reins to haul the big horse in behind the nearest shelter, some brush-screened boulders, a rifle shot lashed and a bullet came whipping viciously into the trail only a matter of a couple of feet behind the horse. Speke was standing close to the black's head now, muttering to the animal, rubbing its nose. He tied the horse to brush, then shucked his coat and flung it across the saddle. He considered the possibility of moving to a place where he could get a safe view up the slopes ahead, from where the shot had come. There was not the slightest doubt in his mind that this was Griffin and Redruth whose possible presence he had been wary of yesterday, but as time had gone by without incident he had tended—obviously unwisely—to lose some of his concentration. Had she known it,

Meg might at last have come out and said he was getting too old for this.

Speke waited, listening. Whoever had shot must have marked the place where the bullet had struck, so would be harbouring no illusions about his having got into cover unscathed. He studied the rise of the land a few yards to his right. He had judged the rifleman to be near to sixty yards ahead and at an elevation of maybe fifty feet. But that, of course, was only one man. The whereabouts of the second one was unknown and that was highly dangerous. If Speke were to make it across to the slope on his right, he might do it without drawing a second shot from the same rifleman, but he might become fatally exposed to the other man's shooting.

It was then that he believed he heard, distantly, a brief exchange, men's voices, with the trick of acoustics which brings clarity of speech from a height to those on lower ground; the word *trail* and the word *left*. One man calling, but not loudly, to another, his clarification of which way the horseman had gone; to the horseman's right, therefore to the shooter's left, off the trail. If one was having to tell the other, it might be assumed that Speke's sudden movements had been seen by only one of them. So, had the second man been unsighted, simply waiting for the rifleman to do the work, or was he in a position where, by chance, he was better able to work his way closer to Speke and most likely get right above him? Speke, because he knew he must make no further mistake anywhere near these two, took the option of waiting for the move that he believed would come; he did go forward for a short distance, still seeking cover, but he now focused his attention on the stony slopes to his right, from which he would be most vulnerable, holding the Winchester in both gloved hands.

A long, hot silence fell. In the throbbing of heat his skin began itching but he remained unmoving. Behind him, beyond the rocks and brush, he could hear the occasional movements and the snuffling of the horse. Sweat gathered on his face and dripped from his jaw, yet still he waited, staring at the slope that went climbing away to join the brassy sky above the tops of the pines. He had all but decided that he had made a mistake when his ear caught some small sounds, and there was the running of loose pebbles.

High above him, emerging from the trees, even as Speke eased his rifle to his shoulder, came Charlie Redruth, rifle in hand and with the attitude of a man stalking a quarry that he had not yet sighted. Speke had no conscience about lining him up. Not long ago, this man's companion—for that was how Speke had worked it out—would have shot him off the horse and then ridden away, of that he felt quite certain.

Speke's Winchester lashed and Redruth was smacked hard by the .44 bullet, rifle falling from his hand, losing his hat, the buff duster flapping as he began sliding, then rolling dustily, gathering speed in a now wild descent, turning over and over, stones coming with him, until he came plunging, then thumping heavily in among boulders at a spot about thirty feet ahead of where Speke was. For a little time small stones continued running, and the dust from Redruth's unchecked passage down the slope hung like whitish smoke, slow to dissipate in the almost windless air.

Speke had levered a fresh round into the chamber. Slowly he began going forward, keeping low, squeezing through a gap between dangerously spiky arms of brush until he came to the place where Redruth was. The buff-coloured duster had spread like the wings of some large bird, Redruth, arms and legs spreadeagled beneath it, lying face down. His ginger hair was thick and unkempt and Speke noticed that the skin of the man's neck was unnaturally pale. Now intent upon locating Griffin, Speke moved on.

His attention now fastened on the place where he had first caught the flash of sun off metal for he was reasoning that, with Redruth trying to work his way into a position above Speke, Griffin would have had no reason to move; but he must have seen Redruth shot and seen his spectacular fall. Speke did not have the desire to remain for much longer in this baking place and was therefore unwilling to leave the next move up to Griffin. First, though, he went back and took a look at the black horse, and found it settled now in spite of the rifle shot from Speke, not far off, followed by the long, tumbling descent of the man, with its attendant shower of small stones.

Speke resolved to delay no longer in taking the game to Griffin who surely could not be in great physical shape after the battering that Speke had given him only hours earlier. So Speke began working his way forward again, knowing the risk of crossing some open spaces. Griffin had the advantage of height. He passed the place where Redruth lay sprawled, then launched himself into the open, running towards a couple of bulky boulders while still trying to keep a watch on the dangerous heights.

Speke arrived behind the larger of the two, then squatted, recovering his breath. He looked critically at the rifle, then briefly drew the Smith and Wesson and checked it. Failure to give the weapons due attention could make the difference between living or dying.

Then he set out at a run for the next cover, some dense green brush. He had to get across some sixty feet and was about half way when he saw the shine of Griffin's face way up the slope, rifle at his shoulder, and the echoing shot came as Speke went diving into what he hoped was concealment even as lethal lead came smashing through branches above him.

At once Speke stood up and fired,

and jacking fast, fired again, seeing dust leap, and Griffin himself go ducking back into cover. That was what Speke wanted. Instead of waiting he went bolting for the next place that looked as though it would offer shelter from above. He arrived near a rough upthrust of rock and at once started shooting again, making small stones fly where he had last seen Griffin. There was a flicker of movement but it was further up, near to the tree-line, so Speke shot again, but knew right off that he had not hit Griffin. What he had done, however, was force the tall man from cover to go seeking other shelter among the stunted pines.

Speke waited, watching carefully; then his ear caught some sounds and he realized that Griffin had got to his horse and was now on the move. Having lost his partner he was pulling out.

Speke stood fully upright, his hard eyes probing the tree-line, and he stayed just as he was until he felt quite certain that Griffin had indeed gone.

SIX

It did not take long for people to stop whatever they were doing, those in the street turning to watch, others being drawn to doorways and to windows. This was in Sabina.

The heavily moustached man, however, astride the dusty black horse, a man in a thigh-length, brown coat and a black, shallow-crowned hat, a bedroll up behind the cantle, the horse slung with capacious saddlebags, looked neither to left nor right as he came walking the mount along the main street.

It was not simply this purposeful, stern-looking horseman, however, who was causing such keen interest, but the fact that he was coming in leading another horse, a roan, which had, slung over its saddle, the body of a man dressed in a filthy, torn duster.

About halfway along the street, the eyes of the solemn rider were none the less alert, though he had been here before and therefore knew exactly where he was going; so when he came nearer to a sign, SABINA COUNTY SHERIFF & TOWN MARSHAL: COUNTY JAIL, he came angling in towards it, towing the captive, nodding roan with its sombre cargo.

A small southerly breeze was stirring dust along the street, filming it across the boardwalks and causing stalks of dry grass on vacant lots to tremble stiffly. Quite aware that his arrival had sparked sharp interest, Speke had not allowed it to affect his single-minded progress. A few of those who had watched him going by came trailing along behind, albeit at a respectful distance, and by the time Speke drew rein and, half turning in the saddle, tugged at the lead to bring the roan closer to the flank of the black, a small but quiet crowd had gathered nearby.

Speke did not dismount but sat staring towards the open door of the county office, from beyond which there were now some stirrings, and the sound of a chair being scraped back. Soon, a middle-sized, plump man in whipcord pants and an ochre-coloured shirt with a grimy badge pinned on the left breast of it, appeared in the doorway. Small eyes in lardy pouches stared back at Speke's and took in the roan horse bearing the duster-clad body that had been brought to his door. This particular peace officer had not been in Sabina the last time Speke had visited, with Meg.

Speke said, 'I'm here to see Jeb Cady on personal business and (jerking his head to indicate the dead man slung across the roan) to return some property of his.'

Clearly not expecting this kind of blunt approach, the plump man swallowed and said, 'Mr Cady, he ain't here right now. Name's Boothby, Sabina County Sheriff.'

Though Speke had the strong belief that

by now this man would know quite well who he was, as indeed would some of the bystanders, he said, 'My name is John Speke. I've got good reason to believe the man I've fetched in here is called Charlie Redruth. He's one of two bastards that shot at me, a dozen miles out, on the trail from Denton. If the other one hadn't turned tail and run, there'd be two horses with dead men on 'em. Jack Griffin, he was, and if he's got any wits at all, he'll still be on the move. Now, where's Jeb Cady?'

How long Cady had been nearby, perhaps only drawn by the still-gathering crowd, Speke did not know, but the marshal now came easing through towards the mounted man. A little older, of course, he had scarcely altered in appearance since Speke had last set eyes on him, the same strikingly handsome face, with only the merest suggestion of looseness beneath the jaw, the same shiny-toothed grin and the customary studied neatness of attire. He had on grey pants, half-boots of good quality, a tan shirt and a light brown hat with a snakeskin band and a wide, stiff-looking brim. Sourly, Speke thought it looked like mail-order.

'I'm right here John. It's been a while. I'm right relieved to see you.' Cady came in close, reached up and grabbed Speke's hand and shook it. He rubbed at the nose of the death-laden roan which had bumped him with its head. 'E-easy,' Cady said. 'E-easy.' Then, 'John, I already heard you've been having some trouble and I was truly sorry to learn about it. I'd like to listen to your side, but not here. Why don't you get down and step inside the office. You can see by the sign that I share this place with Bob Boothby.'

The same easy talk of old, too, Speke thought. But something else was there, something in the eyes—or rather, in back of the eyes—that did not quite match the effortless smoothness of the tongue.

'And *I* already heard you're now the

town marshal,' Speke said, 'but I don't see a badge.'

'No need, John,' said Cady, smiling, 'everybody in Sabina knows who I am. Everybody that matters. Those that don't know find out soon enough.' He turned to Boothby. 'Bob, it would be best if Charlie was taken along to Elney's right away. Tell Elney I'll talk with him later, and Doc Crowther. As the coroner, he'll have to be told.'

Speke said, 'Lump of lead, point four four, out of a Winchester, entry one inch below left rib cage, upward traverse. If he pokes around a while he'll find it's still in there. External injuries sustained as the result of a fall seventy-five feet down a scree slope onto packed earth with stones in it. Charlie was deceased, of course, before he got that far.'

Cady's laugh was a short bark. 'You sure don't change none, John.'

'Oh, I change,' said Speke. 'We all do. But I thought I'd lost the capacity for shock, then found I hadn't.' He swung a long leg back over the cantle and got down, then moved forward to hitch the black to the tie-rail. The roan he had released to be led away by a now bustling, rather fussy Boothby. Speke, observing this, thought it said plenty about Boothby, about where he stood alongside Jeb Cady.

They went on inside the county office where it was marginally cooler, two tall men, one well turned out, one somewhat worn-looking and certainly travel-stained.

'Take a seat, John.'

'I'll stand,' said Speke. 'Right soon, I'm going to seek out some place with a tub. Where's your man Griffin?'

Cady's smile had gone now but he was still affable enough. 'John, I don't know what the hell went on out there—well, all I have is what Jack Griffin said. But it sure is too bad that it's come to this; about Charlie Redruth, I mean.'

'If they hadn't arrived in Denton looking for Harriet and then not taken no for an answer; if they hadn't got their Goddamn' pride stuck halfway down their gullets and taken a shot at me, your Charlie Redruth would still be alive.'

Cady removed his too-good-to-be-true hat and tossed it on Boothby's littered desk and sat down, showing some evidence of weariness. 'It shouldn't have gone the way it did,' he said. 'Sure, I sent them looking for Harriet. John, I didn't know where the hell she'd got to. I told Jack and Charlie to try to locate her, and if they did that, to ask her to come on back to Sabina; and they'd give her safe conduct.' *Safe conduct.* Speke was turning the words over in his mind. Cady said, 'The last thing I'd have expected was that they'd run into you, John.' From the street there came the sound of voices. Somebody called out something indistinguishable, then all fell quiet again. Cady was about to get up from his chair to go take a look when Boothby, his round face flushed, came in. Cady asked, 'What's going on?'

At first Boothby, with a sidelong glance at Speke, seemed not to want to say. Then, 'Couple o' the boys got theirsel's kinda riled up.'

'About what?' asked Cady.

Boothby said, 'About Charlie.'

'Who are they?' Speke asked.

'I don't want no trouble,' Boothby said, real quick. Then, 'Audie Stone, Reb Nickson.'

'Close friends of Redruth's?' Speke asked.

'That's right,' said Boothby. 'Them an' some others in this town. I've told Stone an' Nickson to git off'n the street. They been at the bottle,' he added.

In spite of the bone-aching tiredness he now felt, Speke had wanted to get all of the business concerning Harriet out in the open without undue delay, but Boothby was showing no signs of moving, and he did not consider it any of Boothby's business. To Cady, Speke said, 'You know me well enough by now, Jeb. I won't tolerate being pushed by anybody. You want your streets to stay peaceable, those boys will need to take real good heed of what Sheriff Boothby's told 'em.'

Cady's glance shifted to the county sheriff who probably had no real conception of the true nature of the man in the long coat; and Cady himself could have been in two minds, now, concerning his own position. Speke had been holding something back. Cady could tell that by the way Speke's manner had altered the moment Boothby had come back in, as though he had bitten off his next remark. That meant only one thing. It was very personal. Boothby, however, now that he was here, would not be still.

'There's got to be an inquest held over Mr Redruth.' It was as though he thought that, probably because of what the big man had said, earlier, Speke did not seem to be taking it seriously. So Boothby added the actual words. 'This is a serious business we got here.'

Speke said, 'Mr Boothby, I take being shot at by some demented asshole from nowhere special very seriously indeed. Whether or not it was one or the other that pulled the trigger out there doesn't matter a shit to me.' Then, to Cady, he said, 'Exactly who was Charlie Redruth? *What* was he? A deputy? He didn't have a badge, either.'

A flicker that could have been slight annoyance passed across Cady's face but the easy manner was scarcely disturbed; the surface manner. 'You could say he was a town employee.'

'Employed to do what? Shovel horse-apples?'

'To help me keep order,' Cady said, 'if that became necessary.'

'One of your men, then, like Jack Griffin.'

'Occasional town employees, both,' Cady said, 'but yes, answerable to me, as marshal.'

Boothby's small eyes were shuttling back

and forth between Cady and Speke. It sure was likely that he had never heard Cady talked to the way this big, hard-looking bastard had done today and was therefore waiting for Cady to explode.

Cady in fact did stand up now, but unhurriedly.

'John, I've got things I have to see to because of...what's happened. I know you'll want to talk. That's fine. Right now you look like you need a spell. We can talk plenty later. Come to the house tomorrow. Unless you want to bunk there—and welcome.'

Speke could have pushed it now, but decided not to. He would go along with Cady, just so far. But he said, 'I'll go my own way, Jeb, and I'll come by tomorrow.' He left the office and went down and unhitched the black and remounted. He shuffled the horse away, then turned it and went bobbing along the main street, first to get to a livery, then to a place that had a tub, and to stay overnight.

Going about these tasks did not hold at bay thoughts of Cady and inevitably, fragments of their mutual history. For the first time in a while, the noise and dust and blood and agony of the Hepburn posse came flooding back to Speke. He found that to get rid of it he had consciously to override it.

Sabina itself had certainly grown since Speke had last been here, and though stage lines still fed into the town from more remote places, the well-established railroad had acquired extensive yards and numerous buildings, around which there hung a mixed veil of steam and smoke which gave off a sharp, penetrating smell. And there was most definitely a sense of bustle in many places around Sabina, even though, as everywhere, there was evidence of worklessness, whether by necessity or choice it would have been difficult to say; but the element was there, and any place where it existed had the potential for trouble.

It was on his way back from a livery, his big saddlebags slung over a shoulder, that he became aware of intense scrutiny from several men along the main street, some of whom were sitting on benches, others lounging near saloons. No one said anything but he could feel the animosity, almost as though it was something alive and touchable. Meg's words came back... *'John, for God's sake be careful.'*

SEVEN

Everywhere Speke's eye fell there were pleasant traces of Harriet, from the tasteful prints on the walls to the deeply polished woodwork in this room and the bright covers over sofas and easy chairs. This had been her home.

Jeb Cady had offered him a drink but Speke had declined; a fresher, more alert-looking Speke today, not as well laundered as Cady, to be sure, but clean, and with yesterday's dustiness of clothing brushed away. Now he looked at Cady sitting opposite in a similar deep, comfortable chair.

'There's no use for you and me to go tippy-toed around it, Jeb. It's Harriet I've come about. There's no way I'd choose to mix in your affairs—I mean, in things between you and her, but this is something that can't be left as it is.' He pinned Cady with his dark stare. 'She's not coming back.'

Cady shifted slightly in his seat, recrossed his ankles. These were the only outward signs of his discontent over what Speke had just said to him, but when he spoke his voice held its usual even pitch.

'Harriet is my wife, John, and as my wife, her place is here with me.'

'Harriet's got very good reasons for doing what she did.'

'What can you know about her reasons?' Now Cady did look somewhat disturbed, but only his eyes were giving that away.

Speke well knew that he had to balance what he had come to say against the possibility that out of this so far evenly spoken exchange might suddenly emerge the quite different Jeb Cady; the one that Speke had seen before, on occasions; the one, for example, that had come bursting forth, wide-eyed, during that blazing, dusty fight, when the Hepburn posse had been so badly mauled, the one that had killed without compunction, manacled men, rounding on them like some blood-maddened predator. The law become instant executioner.

'I reckon you know well enough what the reasons are, Jeb. And we've seen the marks.' *Not I but we.*

Cady's face had become quite still, even his eyes unmoving. He allowed several seconds to go by before he said, 'There's always two sides to an argument. There's two sides to this one.'

Speke raised his eyebrows. 'So? Then where are *your* marks, Jeb?'

Cady said, 'We go back a long way, you and me. We had us a few good times and we went through some real bad ones.' If Cady, too, had fleetingly recalled the Hepburn posse he chose not to single it out, perhaps for the very reason that had come most clearly to Speke's mind. Equally, if he was seeking to establish a more comfortable, more sympathetic base from which to carry on this discussion, it was plain from Speke's iron face that this was not about to happen. Cady picked that up soon enough so did not waste any more time pursuing it. 'Harriet,' he said, 'can be real hard to live with.'

But Speke had had enough. 'Don't talk that kind of shit, Jeb, not to me. I've told you, I've seen the marks on that woman. Meg's seen them. That was the reason I wouldn't allow Griffin and Redruth to take her anywhere. Those two roosters came into the Alonquin in Denton with pistols pulled. That was the only reason they got her out of the building. That was their way of *asking* her to come back to Sabina. That was the offer of safe conduct. The first chance I got I bent a barrel over Charlie Redruth's head and then beat the shit out of your other man, Jack Griffin. Did you know he kind of fancies himself with his hands? Anyway, that's how come the pair of 'em were waiting for me. They knew that sooner or later I'd be along, because they were supposed to be carrying that as a message to you. That was my mistake, but I got it half squared in the finish. So I'll say it to you again, Jeb: she's not coming back.'

Now Cady stood up and went pacing around the room, whether merely to gather his thoughts or to control his temper, Speke was not quite able to decide. But Speke had come to this house today unarmed, a gesture maybe, a silent statement that in spite of the unwelcome message he bore, he still believed that a rational discussion was possible, even allowing Cady's history. But in coming, he had chosen not to leave Cady in any doubt as to the certainty of Harriet's break with him or his personal disquiet over her treatment at Cady's hands. And the only way Speke had been able to do that had been with bluntness. Surprisingly, when Cady settled down again, though he did not go back to his chair, there was no evidence of mounting anger, rather more of conciliation; even contrition.

'Right, John, seeing it's you and me here, we can talk freely. I reckon I've done well, over these past few years anyway.' He made a general gesture with a hand. 'This place shows it. This is where Harriet's home is. But, by God, it's not been easy. This town was growing fast—maybe too fast—and a few things were starting to get out of hand. When it comes to the pinch, Bob Boothby's not the man he needs to be. That's the main reason I'm the town marshal and not the mayor. Sabina had got to the stage where it needed a real firm hand. Investors don't put money into any place that can't keep order.' So far there was nothing that Speke could have quarrelled with; and he did not believe that Cady was simply seeking to inflate his own part in what had happened in Sabina. On the contrary, Speke could readily believe what that had probably entailed, for in the past he had found himself in similar situations. Cady seemed to be gathering himself in order to go on. 'I'll not pretend to you, or anybody, that in getting it done, taking a firm hand here, I wasn't looking out for my own interests as well. And I've sure made mistakes. And sometimes (nodding to encompass the house they were in), it could get kind of, well, worked up. But it wasn't all one way, John. Not all one way.'

'She's been *hit*, Jeb, hit hard and often. So don't let's shit around. Hit enough to send you the message that she's not coming back. If that was one of your *mistakes* it was a big one, and it can't be set right. Not now.'

That Cady was now decidedly uncomfortable was quite clear, and an old-time flash of animation came. 'Where the hell could she go?'

Speke provided an answer that was not necessarily the true one, but it would give Cady something to think about. 'With me and Meg, maybe. We've not got to that yet. Harriet's not been well enough.'

Cady took another turn around the room. 'She's still in Denton?'

'She was when I left, but she'll be gone by this.'

'Gone where?'

'That's for her and Meg to decide.'

'So when you leave here, how will you get to know where they are?'

'There'll be word left for me in Denton. For me, not for anybody else that comes sniffing. We've had our fill of Griffins and Redruths.'

Cady turned to face Speke again. 'So is that it, John? That's what you've come here to tell me, and you'll go now?' He must have known that it was by no means all that Speke had come for.

'There's still the matter of what's owed to Harriet.' He sure did not need to explain that, for it was knowledge that Cady would accept that Speke possessed. But Speke added, 'That money that was hers to begin with, and whatever the profits from it are, that she'll be entitled to.'

Cady stood still, looking at him steadily, and presently said, 'It was Harriet walked out of here, not me.'

'In my view it's not relevant.'

'In your view.'

'You want attorneys to test it, she'll go that far.'

'And meantime, John, you're her adviser?'

'I'm the man who's suggested to her it would be better all round if attorneys could be kept out of it.'

Cady drew in a long breath. Maybe he no longer trusted himself to keep his temper reined in. 'This is something I'm going to have to think about.'

'Then, my advice is, don't take too long.'

'You seem to be turning into a general adviser, and that's not like you.'

'I've changed,' said Speke, 'whether for the better or worse isn't for me to say.' He knew he did not have to spell out again what it was that had wrought in him this particular change. Again he said, 'Don't be too long about it, Jeb. She'll be waiting for an answer.'

'I don't take kindly to being pushed either. Of all people you should know that.'

'To a point we're two of a kind,' said Speke easily. 'We both know that. That's why this talk can be plain. I'd have got it all said yesterday around at that office but Boothby came back in. It's between you and me, on Harriet's behalf, and we can keep it that way.' Cady nodded slowly as though acknowledging the fact readily enough, though Speke could read him sufficiently to know that the other man's mind would be racing now, testing all kinds of possibilities. Which no doubt was another reason that Cady had asked for time to think. 'How much time?' Speke asked.

Cady said, 'Give me today, John. We'll talk some more tomorrow.'

'No longer?'

Cady shook his head. 'No longer.'

Speke stood and picked up his hat, and asked something else that he needed to know. 'Where's Jack Griffin?'

'Not in town,' Cady said. 'We thought it wouldn't do anybody any good to have him still here when you came in. Too much hot blood.'

Now, there was an irony, thought Speke, but he merely nodded and said, 'Just so long as he stays out of my sight.' Then, 'What about Redruth?'

Cady made a quick, impatient gesture. 'Like Jack, Charlie Redruth was a fool. If he'd just come on back to Sabina he'd be alive now.' Speke had cause to wonder about such a readily dismissive remark but let it go.

'This Boothby, is he going to see it that way?'

'Yes,' said Cady, 'he is.' That seemed to nail down Cady's influence in this place.

Speke walked to the door, Cady coming out on the porch with him. A man Speke had not seen before was approaching, a weedy-looking individual wearing a store suit and a derby hat.

'Mr Cady?'

'What is it, Cobb?'

'Feller that come off the Laskey train, he's causin' a real ruckus up at Helvig's.'

'What for? What kind of ruckus?'

'Claims people paid for land here in the county, an' it don't exist.'

Speke could read nothing from Cady's expression but things that Harriet had said were sure coming back.

Cady said, 'Go tell Helvig I'll come on down.'

'Tomorrow then,' said Speke. He went pacing away, Cady going back inside to get his hat and, presumably, a firearm.

When Speke got as far as the main street, however, he was in no great hurry, and waited until he saw Cady, on foot, emerge from Fremont and go heading away, angling across towards a bold red and white sign among many others: LAND OFFICE:

ARN D. HELVIG: REAL ESTATE.

An old man at a tie-rail, adjusting the cinches on a thin, sad-looking sorrel, was also observing the marshal's progress, but gave Speke a sidelong glance.

'You're the feller brung in the dead man.'

'The same,' said Speke.

The old man raked fingers at his grey whiskers. 'Name's Boland. Harry Boland. Got to say yuh done a good thing. Few other parties might reckon so an' all, but not come right out an' say so.' He sniffed, tilting his head back. 'John Speke. Well now.'

'I take it you weren't a friend of Charlie Redruth's?'

Boland spat in the dry street. 'Soon as bump knees with a black widder.'

'I hear there's high voices been heard up at Helvig's,' Speke ventured.

'Ah,' said Boland, 'so that's what's up.' He stood squinting after Cady.

'You're a Sabina man then?'

'I'm from here an' there,' Boland said. 'Here an' there. Ranch work, minin' up in the Case Ranges one time. Even worked in a railroad gang, once.'

Speke moved on, not waiting for any visible outcome to Cady's visit to Helvig's but he noticed that the old man was still hanging around, watching.

For reasons that Speke could not even begin to understand he had the feeling that the hours between now and when next he was to talk with Cady were going to seem interminable.

EIGHT

Speke had eaten a leisurely supper at the hotel he had checked into, the Haddon House; then, selecting a cigar from a slim case that he reached from an inside pocket, he went out to take a turn around the Sabina streets. Though he did not particularly expect trouble, in view of his relationship with Cady, he had buckled on the Smith and Wesson, but his thigh-length coat concealed it; and he had arranged matters so that the pistol was on his left hip, handle foremost, so that the flick of a coat-button with the fingers of his left hand would allow the coat to fall open for an unimpeded cross draw.

As he strolled he called at the livery to check on the black horse, then went on, passing from time to time under pole-hung street lanterns and going by lighted stores, familiarizing himself again with the centre of the town, looking at places that were new since the last time he had been here. He passed long-established buildings too, the telegraph office, the newspaper, the Sabina County Speaker and, leaving the main street, traversing less-lit ways, the railroad depot, a spider's web of tracks glinting in the yards there; and against the evening sky, the bulky shape of the water tower. Traders' signs were everywhere. There was wealth to be had here for those with money to invest and for those fortunate enough to own real estate.

Speke went pacing back in the direction of the main street, Pitman, discarding the stub of his cigar as he went. The day had been hot, and some of that gathered-up heat remained in the air and the structures that he passed, for there was little breeze. To the south, drawn against the cloudless sky were the jagged shapes of the Case Ranges, their lower reaches riven with dry canyons, while, as he knew, to the south-west lay the Calley Flats and the curve of the Sabina River that Harriet had mentioned in regard to the wagon-family, and which still teased at Speke's mind.

Strolling by a lightless lumber yard, Speke's attention was seized by some kind of activity near the end of this sidestreet, not far from where it joined the lamp-glow of Charleston, so that looking towards it from deeper darkness, Speke was aware of spidery figures limned against the lighter place.

A cry came, high-pitched, then a louder, deeper shout of alarm and some cursing, the several men involved quite obviously struggling, fighting. Speke's swift release of the button allowed his coat to swing free and he began lengthening his stride. Another cry went up, a cry that was abruptly cut short, then men were running, Speke himself now jogging towards someone who appeared to have fallen.

The man was lying huddled near a tall board fence some thirty feet short of the corner of Charleston, and by the time Speke got to him, no one else was around. Down on one knee, Speke struck a match, and by its flare and yellow flickering, saw a man of about middle age, dressed in a grey, city suit, a dark-coloured derby lying near him, blood and dirt on the man's face and dust all over his clothing. From the corner, on Charleston, somebody called, 'What's goin' on?'

'There's a man been hurt,' Speke answered.

'Wait...' Whoever it had been went away.

A doctor did not come, but among others, a druggist named Osborne did, a plump man in a white, button-to-the-neck druggist's coat, and eye-glasses. Other men had brought a lantern.

The druggist took a detailed look at the man slumped on the ground, who was now making small movements and some

134

whimpering noises.

'Somebody sure worked him over,' Osborne commented, and glanced up meaningfully at Speke.

'No,' said Speke, 'it wasn't me, but I heard it, and from along there I saw what was happening. Some men left in a hurry. Maybe they heard me coming.'

Osborne grunted and resumed his examination of the injured man, at the same time asking him who he was and where he lived. Presently the druggist looked up. 'Nothing broken so far as I can tell, but he needs some treatment and some cleaning up. Says his name's Wells and he's at the Haddon House.' To the men who had come, he said, 'Let's get him as far as the drugstore. I'll treat his cuts and then he can go back to the hotel.'

Right about then Cady came striding up and it all had to be said over again, and Cady said, 'Mr Wells. Yes, we met just today. He's in Sabina on business.' In the wavery, buttery lanternlight Cady gave Speke a probing look. 'It seems you happened along at just the right time, John.' Speke nodded. Leaning down, Cady then asked Wells, 'Mr Wells, what can you tell me about those men?'

Wells, through swollen lips, said something that sounded like *drunks* and Cady sighed and straightened up. 'Yes, well...this sort of thing does Sabina no good at all, Mr Wells being a visitor here. I'll make all the enquiries I can. John...?'

Speke shook his head. 'Not close enough, but I'm near to certain there were three of 'em.' And he added slowly, 'For drunks they were moving real good.'

Wells was raised up by a couple of men and supported away, Cady and the others following. All but Speke and one other. Once the small bunch was out of earshot, Boland said, 'That there was the rooster that was kickin' up all the shindy at Helvig's. Seen 'im come outa there with Jeb Cady.'

'What was the problem?' Speke asked.

'Heard he come about land that was sold elsewhere. Land reckoned to be in Sabina County, mostly on Calley Flats. An' about some pilgrims that come here expectin' land, an' left, an' never showed up no more.'

'How do you know this, Harry?'

'About Wells? Aw, it come out soon enough, from one o' Helvig's own clerks. Helvig sure got his dander up. Claimed this Wells was accusin' him o' fraud. Cady got it all calmed down.' Then, as though suddenly apprehensive, Boland glanced around. Though no one else could be seen nearby it was obvious to Speke that the old man had now become jittery, maybe not wanting to be seen in a long conversation with him, or maybe because Speke was known to be close to authority in this town. Speke said, 'Did you see Wells attacked?'

'Nope. Saw 'em comin' with the lantern, is all.'

'Harry,' Speke said, 'for what it's worth,

it wasn't me attacked Wells. But I intend having a word with him. And I'm not one of Cady's men. I've known Jeb a long time, but I found out recently I didn't know him as well as I'd thought.'

After a moment or two Boland said, 'I got to step careful, Speke.'

'Why?'

'Same reason as this Wells feller come here. Same reason another feller come a while back, lookin' fer them folks that last got scammed on a land deal.'

'They came in a wagon?'

Boland's eyes glittered under shaggy brows. 'What d'yuh know about that?' The edginess was back.

'What word I got was from Mrs Harriet Cady,' Speke said. 'My...wife's sister. It's on her behalf that I'm here at all. She's left Cady.'

'By God!' Boland said, surprised and sounding much relieved about Speke.

'Another man came...' Speke prompted. He wanted to pursue this now, nothing specific in mind, merely a scarcely formed notion that there might turn out to be something in it that he could turn to advantage on Harriet's behalf. After all, that had been the incident that had triggered some of Cady's final violence against her.

'A man, a woman an' a child come in the wagon. They had what they thought was a title to land down on Calley Flats. River land. They'd paid their money over but the title was worth nothin'. It's happened to other folks. But that last feller, he headed off an' he swore he'd find out who it was played him fer a fool. An' he did say he'd got a few ideas about it.'

'So he and his family pulled out.'

'Yep. He did have some sort o' ruckus with one o' Cady's men though. That Jack Griffin as I recall.' Boland paused for a few seconds. ''Bout a day after that, I was headin' out towards the Case Ranges, takin' supplies to a feller that was prospectin' out there at the time. I reckon

I seen the wagon. It was a long ways off. Watched it near out of sight. Couldn't figure it nohow.'

'How so?'

'Wrong direction,' Boland said. 'Headin' due south. Warn't the way he'd said he'd come. Warn't the way he oughta been headin', goin' out.'

'And you?'

'Me? South-west, I was goin'; so in the finish I lost sight of it.'

'Maybe he just changed his mind.' Speke thought he had said something of the sort to Harriet.

'Nothin' to take the man that way, not with a woman an' child. Bad stretch o' country. Only a few fools lookin' to find silver ore that warn't there. When I made a camp I could hear some o' that on the wind; a blast or two in the canyons. Near to sundown, that was. Anyways, about that wagon. Feller that claimed to be some kin to the woman, he come to Sabina. He'd expected to meet 'em on their land, on

Calley Flats. I did hear that Cady made enquiries on the telegraph fer that feller, but they come to nothin'.'

'So now Wells has come.'

'He sure has.'

'Did you tell anybody about seeing the wagon?'

'Nope.'

'Why not, Harry?' Speke thought he knew the answer already, though.

'Warn't none o' my Goddamn' business. Anyways, there was other wagons around. I couldn't've swore it was theirs.'

Speke thought it best not to press the matter. In his time, Harry Boland might have accumulated good reasons for not asking too many questions or giving out information around Sabina. They walked on now. Before they reached the Charleston corner, where the lights were, Boland mumbled goodnight and split away from Speke, maybe, thought Speke, regretting having said as much as he had, and to a stranger.

141

Speke walked back to the Haddon House, but just short of it, encountered Cady, who had been in conversation with a pair of hard-looking, rangy individuals, both of whom gave Speke deliberate scrutiny as they moved away.

'Some more of your people?' Speke enquired mildly.

'No,' said Cady, 'but men to steer clear of. Red Nickson and Audie Stone.'

'Sober now,' Speke commented. 'The friends of Charlie Redruth.' He wondered if Cady's remark had been intended to carry a warning. 'Seems the marshal's got his finger on the pulse of the town. That can't be a bad thing.'

'They're a pair of wild ones,' Cady said. 'You heading back to the Haddon House?'

'I am.' And he added deliberately, 'Could be I'll offer Mr Wells a word or two of comfort when he comes back to the hotel.'

'I'd leave it, John,' said Cady quietly.

Wells is a man who brings accusations but no facts to back them. It's too bad he got jumped like that, but he's leaving Sabina real soon.'

Speke merely nodded, bade Cady goodnight and walked on; yet he knew that Cady was watching him every step of the way to the Haddon House.

Boland, too, was being watched but he did not know it; just as he had been watched earlier while in conversation with the big man who had fetched Charlie Redruth in, dead. John Speke.

NINE

The room, ill-lit, stank of formaldehyde,
lye soap and sweat, and there were other
smells less readily identifiable but no
less unpleasant. Six men were in there,
counting the deceased laid out naked
on Elney's table, Elney himself, tall
and spare, overseeing; a doctor named
Crowther, Sheriff Boothby, Jeb Cady and
Speke. Speke, because while standing near
an open window at the Haddon House,
he had heard a man's voice among
others, say, 'Dump the bastard here.'
Whoever they were they had been in
an unkempt vacant lot behind the hotel.
Speke, at the time seeking some relief
in the seemingly airless room, had been
talking with the battered and cowed
Wells.

Now that Crowther, having made an examination of the corpse, straightened, his shadow leaping against the dirty ceiling, they could all observe the full horror before them.

'It's my opinion,' Crowther said, 'that he suffered cardiac failure induced by what was being done to him.'

Boothby's face was so drained of colour that it seemed transparent and he looked as though his greatest wish was to get out of this terrible room as soon as he possibly could.

Cady was staring at the laid-out body, solemn but unreadable. Speke's moustached face was like granite, offering no reflection of the deep anger that was raging in him.

Elney, in his incongruously high voice, said, 'I understand his name was Boland.'

Nobody contradicted him. They were still thinking over Crowther's words, *what was being done to him,* the ghastly results of which were all too plain, the swollen,

145

hideously blistered genitals, scarcely recognizable for what they were, all pubic hair burned off. Boland looked as though he had had that part of his anatomy dipped in acid, but these burns had been made by flames. Finally Boothby said what must have been in other minds.

'He musta...made one hell of a noise...'

Crowther's examination, however, had yielded an answer to that. 'There are signs that something, probably a leather strap, had been fastened around his mouth at some stage, and there are fibres caught between one or two of his teeth. I'd say a cloth was pushed into his mouth and held in there quite tightly with the strap.'

Elney waved a spidery hand. 'The few dollars in bills and coin that he had on him are over there on that shelf.'

Boothby cleared his throat. 'Boland owned an old sorrel horse. That's got to be around town somewhere.' Then, 'Why would anybody want to do that to him?' He must have known that he was not about to get an answer; or maybe he knew what the answer was and did not expect to hear it.

Speke turned his hard face to Boothby and something in the stare that he gave the Sabina County lawman caused Boothby to look away.

Cady said, 'There's no more to be done here.' But to Elney, he added, 'We'll see what can be got for his belongings when we find them, to take care of your costs.'

Speke left ahead of anyone else, not trusting himself to say anything. Outside, near Elney's door, he pushed his way past a couple of loungers, Stone and Nickson, these men perhaps drawn by recent activities. Stone muttered something to Speke's back and Speke turned fast to confront him. Speke's own words were softly delivered but there could be no mistaking the menace, the barely reined-in violence lying at back of them.

'I did hear tell that you pair of tinplate hard men wanted a word with me over what happened to that bastard Redruth. Well, here I am, boys, and Elney's got room enough for more in there on his table.' Speke's coat had swung open, the sweetly curved handle of the Smith and Wesson jutting from his left hip. In the space of a blink he had become all that they had likely heard about him, not simply the hard man who had ridden, long ago, courting death, with Jeb Cady, but *the pistolman, John Speke,* and even these two, unused to being faced down, hesitated.

During that hesitation Cady came out and stopped abruptly, his eyes flicking between them and Speke. The men nodded curtly to the marshal and walked away. Watching them go, even Cady seemed to be somewhat relieved. Speke wondered if he himself was allowing his short-acquaintance dislike of them to influence his thinking. Or had he smelled woodsmoke on them? But he said, 'Tomorrow morning then, Jeb.' He, too, walked on, heading back to the Haddon House but hearing Boothby emerging from Elney's to join Cady, and he could almost feel their eyes on his back as he went.

Back in his hotel room he shucked coat and pistol but did not immediately turn in. Instead, he sat on the edge of the bed, closed his eyes briefly and made a conscious effort to settle his breathing, for he was still trying to control the anger that had flooded him while viewing the sad, wasted, tormented remains of Harry Boland, an individual he had been aware of for a paltry few days. And Speke's anger now was the product, the fusion of more than one offensive matter. The core of it, of course, was the treatment that he knew Harriet to have received at the hands of Jeb Cady, Harriet, a woman without the strength even to begin defending herself But there were other strands to his anger; the cheating of ordinary people who had put their trust in others, over land, the savage treatment of the investigator, Wells, a man clearly out of his depth, the attempted murder of Speke himself, and now the brutal affair of the old and defenceless Boland. And Harry Boland had died, so Speke was now convinced, while men in Sabina had been intent on discovering what connection there might be between Boland and Speke, and indeed what might have passed between them. So Speke was now tending to lay the blame at his own door. The question was, of course, who were they and what was it that had made them so desperate to find out what Boland and Speke might have talked about? Stone and Nickson sprang at once to mind. A third man, if they had been the same ones that had attacked Wells. Griffin? Wherever he was, Speke had not seen a whisker of him.

Wells was a badly frightened man, and consequently Speke had been able to learn little from him beyond the name of the family he had been trying, albeit clumsily, to trace, and that was Hagen; and the fact that the man who had earlier come looking for them, the woman's brother, was no longer fit enough to make a second journey. And yes, the men who had attacked him, three of them, had smelled strongly of liquor, but had not uttered a word other than a curse or two. The yelling had come from Wells himself. Speke, however, had asked one or two final questions, among them, 'When the other man came here, the woman's brother, how was he treated? By Boothby? By Jeb Cady?'

'Boothby I don't know. To me, he only mentioned Cady. He said Cady used the telegraph, asking around different places but he got no answers.'

Speke had not been able to get much more than that. Through his swollen lips Wells had said that there was a train through Sabina tomorrow, going in the direction he wanted, and by God he planned to be on it. Speke had emerged with an impression that Wells was a man who had manifestly oversold his capabilities to whoever was paying him for his enquiries.

Speke removed his boots, then spread a newspaper on the floor, and kneeling, carefully checked and cleaned the Smith and Wesson. While he was engaged in that task he thought about Harriet and about Meg, waiting in Denton, and how seriously Meg would now be counselling him had she known what was going through his mind. *'Leave it, John. For God's sake leave it. Do what you can for Harriet, then come away. Come back.'* He knew her so well that he could almost hear her soft voice saying it. Then oddly, he wondered if, in his absence, they had talked of him. Might Meg, with her vague concerns, have tried to *sound Harriet out?* Her sister. Close. Even closer now, because of all this sorry business. Speke stood up, wiping his large hands on a cloth. Tomorrow he would front Cady once again, try to force the issue. He glanced down at his clothing, realizing that he had brought with him some of the odours of Elney's back room. The smell of death.

Today, an undersized, round, bald man with a parrot-beak of a nose was with Cady. Soderman. It was kind of early in the day, Speke thought, for a banker to be out.

Soderman sat in one of the deep, comfortable chairs, his boots just brushing the floor, and he was massaging the fingers of one pudgy hand with the other. When Speke came in, carrying his hat, Soderman stared at him in what seemed to be momentary apprehension, and thereafter scarcely took his attention away from the big man. Speke wondered idly what the banker had been told about him. Speke unbuttoned his coat before he sat down, exposing the left-carried pistol, and in so doing, probably did little for Soderman's peace of mind. None the less the banker cleared his throat, and by way of explanation or excuse, said, 'Mr Cady has asked that I be on hand today, Mr Speke, to offer a financial opinion to do with, er, your discussions.'

Which meant, Speke assumed, that Soderman or more likely his bank had an interest in some of Cady's assets and had now been thrown this unwanted complication. Banks did not like complications.

'That's up to Mr Cady,' said Speke. 'I've only come here for an answer.'

Cady said, 'Well John, I'm sure you can appreciate it isn't quite as cut and dried as that.'

'I had a notion that it wouldn't be,' said Speke.

Soderman gave a sharp, dry cough. 'It is a question,' he said, 'of liquidity. Partly. There is also the problem of assessing the true value of Mrs Cady's, er, share...her reasonable expectations based on the amount of capital which she, er, contributed at the outset.'

Speke now thought that Cady must have

been saving the expense of an attorney by having this little mealy-mouthed money man talking for him, so he asked bluntly: 'What did Harriet put in, Jeb; was it half of what you had to start with? Was it three-parts? Was it nine-tenths? I never did hear, but that's surely at the heart of it.'

Soderman and no doubt Cady could easily see where that was going to lead, so it was the banker who said quickly, 'Mr Speke, that is not as relevant as it might seem. What has to be taken into account is *how* the money—whatever the amount was—was, er, used to fund, er, acquisitions and generate further sums, and at what rate, er, over time. And with what skills, which are not easily measurable.'

Abruptly Speke said, 'Jeb, why not just settle for fifty-fifty?'

He thought Soderman was about ready to choke. Cady smiled with his mouth, his eyes fastened on Speke in a flat, dead manner.

'Is that it? Is that what she sent you here to say? Fifty-fifty?'

'Apportionment wasn't even mentioned,' said Speke truthfully, 'only facts. Only history. The history of Harriet's money, right at the start. Without it there really could have been no start.'

Cady's voice was perfectly steady when he said, 'Whatever settlement is reached, I think that Harriet herself ought to be part of the discussions.'

'I do agree, Mr Cady,' Soderman said. He had begun to sweat slightly and now tended to look away whenever Speke's big, ravaged face turned towards him.

'I've said it before, Jeb,' said Speke, 'it's me or it's an attorney. Finally it could go to a court of law. Who would want all kinds of private affairs coming out in a court?' Speke knew quite well that this was ground that Cady would by no means wish to tread while Soderman was present. Cady said, still in a calm, reasonable tone, 'John, it must seem like

I'm putting you off, playing for time, but just as Mr Soderman has said, there's a whole lot to be taken into account here. Like it or not, it's complicated. Look, I want to suggest that you go on back to...to wherever Harriet is, and assure her that what she wants has been heard and that we're going to try real hard to work out what's fair. What do you say?'

'I'd say that Mr Soderman, here, from Sabina's biggest bank, has got access to an attorney who can advise on the sort of law that fits this. That doesn't mean that an attorney has to *come in*. I know damn' well it's complicated, but before I leave Sabina I've got to have an agreement to show to Harriet, a binding agreement, all written down and signed and witnessed. I'm going to wait around a day or two longer to give you time—and Mr Soderman time—to have that drawn up. At this stage money doesn't have to change hands, just an undertaking that will hold, in law, and a deadline to get it all sewn up.'

'Um... intent... yes. Yes,' muttered Soderman.

'You're driving a damn' hard bargain for her, John,' Cady said, his control now showing signs of fraying.

'I didn't come all this way to do anything less.' Speke stood up. 'This is the last delay though. If I come back one more time Jeb, only to get put off, then I'll go back and advise Harriet to hire an attorney. Meg and I will stay with her, see her through it. For as long as it takes.' Cady now looked as though he would have liked to have gotten rid of Soderman in order to talk with Speke alone, but Speke could perceive no profit in that, so moved to the door. 'I'll be back in a day. Two, maybe. No more.' He left.

By the time he walked out on the street he had made up his mind about something else and was trying to shut out Meg's voice, sounding inside his head. Less than an hour later, mounted on the black horse, which sure was looking for the exercise, he was heading out of Sabina, westwards, a bedroll up, a canteen, his Winchester scabbarded, thinking wryly that for somebody who was widely known as a pistolman, of late he seemed to have been putting a whole lot of faith in the rifle.

Five miles out of Sabina he changed direction, heading due south.

TEN

Boland had said *south*, the wagon had been heading, while Boland himself had been going southwest and thus, on a divergent line, the distance between the old man and the wagon increasing as each minute passed. Speke therefore had made his own observations based on what he had been told and was now on a line-of-ride taking him due south of Sabina towards the canyons on the fringes of the Case Ranges which, today, were rising purple-shadowed against a delft-blue sky.

This was difficult country, in parts flat and dusty, in others scattered with upthrusts of ancient rocks and clumped here and there with wind-stunted trees and hardy brush. Thus, though on several occasions he paused to regard his back-trail,

Speke could by no means be certain that, perhaps having been seen leaving Sabina, he had not been followed. He had been able to discern no rise of dust or flash of metal, but that, as he knew, meant very little.

Later in the day, coming down a scree slope into a greener area of bunch grass, he came upon a small creek running shallowly but clearly over a stony bottom, and near this he dismounted and made a camp. Considering the question of lighting a fire he decided he would do so. If no one was near, then it would not be seen. If he *had* been followed, then avoiding a fire would be pointless.

He rustled up a quantity of dry sticks and soon had bacon sizzling and coffee bubbling. The ride had given him an appetite, and after he had allowed the black horse to drink at the creek and led it back to be picketed nearby, he sat down and ate his meal.

Once or twice during this ride he had

gone back over his motives for making it and had come to a belief that somewhere out here lay the answer to the puzzle of what had become of the wagon family whose last human contact had been, ostensibly, with persons in Sabina. With Cady, for one. With Helvig, the real estate man, for another. Harriet had been disquieted about them and had paid a price for that.

Speke himself was now well aware of the kind of men to be found in Sabina and had indeed come close to being badly wounded or even killed on his way to that place. Cady was the enigma. There had been times when, during their talks, Speke had almost come to believe in the man's contrition, while at others he had caught flashes of the other Cady, the one that he already knew existed but which was most often concealed, certainly shielded from public exposure. Cady had done well, there could be no denying that, but his rule of law, Speke thought, had been a brutal one, carried out at arm's length by some very dangerous men. True, it could be argued, as Cady did, that in places such as Sabina, a firm hand was often necessary; and Speke had not been able to quarrel with that view, that investors would always shy away from those places which could not maintain law in the community. Yet, as Speke also knew, there was all too often a fine dividing line between the keeping of law and order and a policy of strong-arm policing. Sometimes, indeed, the practitioners developed a taste for it, for the heady sense of power and for the rewards that so often flowed from power. So a possible answer to questions about the town of Sabina and the county surrounding it, and those holding power there, had begun to form in his mind; but that, for the moment, was all that it was, a *possible* answer, speculation. Yet he had not been able to overcome the grinding anger that had been building in him between the time he had seen the ugly bruising to Harriet's body, and looking at the poor, pathetic remains of the old man, Harry Boland, laid out in Elney's sombre back room.

Speke dozed, awakened, listening, dozed again, and before sunup, stiff, his joints cracking, stood and walked around, restoring his circulation. Meg had already hinted that she thought he was too old for the sort of life he continued to lead. Dear, loving, irritating Meg. Now he brought her face into focus and longed to be able to say to her, *'No, Megs, there was nothing, ever, between Harriet and me.'* And he thought, *'If we'd brought it out in the open, between us, it could have been buried long since.'* But people tend not to deal with such things with that level of wisdom. Why? Fear of hearing the worst? A desire to hold something back, hold it in reserve for a time when accusing words might be needed? He wondered if, by now, she might actually have put it to Harriet openly.

Speke led the black horse to the water again, then gathered his belongings and prepared to push on. The deeply creviced country was before him and it was there that his hopes now lay. No, not his hopes, his apprehensions.

A couple of miles beyond the creek he came to a narrow canyon whose entrance was all but blocked by what obviously were very old rockfalls, and he made no attempt to go in. Instead he moved on and for the next three hours made searches further south-east. When he paused to rest he stood studying more of the rocky, riven places, now almost conceding the futility of the task he had set for himself and right now he would have given a lot for some of the shrewd, old-prospector knowledge of the likes of Harry Boland.

He was considering whether or not he ought simply to return to Sabina and concentrate on the business he had gone there for in the first place. Out here there were too many possibilities, the task too great. And maybe Boland had been mistaken. The wagon he had seen might not have been the one that had pulled out of Sabina with the Hagens on board. This was a huge country. People could get swallowed up in its vastness. Speke pressed large fingers into the small of his back, then remounted. A sun-shadowed slit of a canyon lay about a quarter of a mile from where he was now. He would ease on down and take a look, maybe even pause for some grub, then head on out.

Fifty yards into the baking, windless place he could see some evidence of past habitation, an old trail faintly marked, some tumble-down, age-grey structures, some pieces of rusted implements; but another hundred yards on, there were a few shacks that looked to be less time- and weather-ravaged.

This had clearly been the scene of a mining operation—or at least exploration—maybe where miners had been based. Boland had said something about men looking for ore that wasn't there. So this must be one of the almost countless places where men had sought the hard earth's riches only to move on, defeated and disillusioned, leaving behind them the flaking detritus of their tenancy.

Over centuries rocks had come tumbling down onto the floor of this great split in the earth. Wild weeds and tough brush had grown among them and had somehow survived, but there was about the place an air of desolation, a sense of defeat, the triumph of the raw land over mere humanity.

Speke, himself feeling depressed, might have pulled out then, heading back towards Sabina, but as he sat the standing horse, idly rubbing at its neck, his attention became engaged by a rockfall some fifty yards to his right, a huge slide of stone that had come from the wall of the canyon. For several minutes he sat studying it, intrigued by the fact that immediately above the fan of scree and boulders, the indentation in the canyon's wall was unusual. The places from where the rock had been dislodged bore sooty streaks and faint yellowish patches. Something else that Boland had said to him now came back and with a ringing clarity, about hearing at least one explosion, and the old man's assumption was that it had been caused by miners. Certainly, this fall was not particularly old. It had not developed much plant-growth in the silty, wind-blown soil that was mixed in among the rocks.

Speke kneed the black and unhurriedly guided it nearer, then stopped once again. About halfway up jutted a big rock which was obviously supporting a whole heap of smaller ones. Speke thought it over for a few minutes more, then turned the horse around and walked it carefully across the rough floor of the canyon and eventually, passing among low brush and rusting iron, circled the four shacks which were spaced a few yards apart and in a line, each with a lean-to at its back. There were two tipped-over structures that had been outhouses.

It was several minutes before he found what he was looking for among numerous discarded implements, a pickaxe, still intact, its steel head covered with gingery surface rust but its hickory handle in good order. Speke swung down and retrieved it. He tied the black in under a lean-to and loosened the cinches and slipped the bit. He slung his coat down, then carrying the pick, walked back the way he had come, returning to the base of the rock-slide.

Speke had decided that, to assuage his curiosity, he would spend an hour or two attempting to undermine the very large and obviously heavy rock. If he were to be successful and could get himself out of the way in good time, he might dislodge enough rock to be able to find out what, if anything, lay behind it. He had now come to believe that it had been caused deliberately and could think of no reason why this should be so.

First taking a long look around, he grasped the pick firmly, then with some difficulty began working his way up the slope, sometimes balancing awkwardly, dislodging stones, until at last he came level with the big, protruding rock, and once in position, set about swinging the pick, attacking the underpinning of trapped, smaller stones.

By the time the sun had passed beyond the canyon's western rim, sweating, his muscles protesting, his breathing fiery in his throat, Speke had cut in sufficiently, sending head-sized rocks skittering down, to pause and re-examine the big one and try to gauge when it might fall away. That would be a moment fraught with danger, for he was now balanced precariously and might easily be swept away. Though his hands were sore he took a fresh grip of the hickory and again began swinging the pick. Ten minutes later he saw a small, abrupt movement of the big rock and he went clambering to one side, then, hurling the pick down ahead of him, went half running, crunching among stones, feeling the edge of the slide moving under him, and finally came staggering onto the canyon floor, the roar of the sliding rocks gathering at his back.

The torrent of rock was roaring like a grey waterfall, dust rising and spreading until eventually a near-silence fell, merely the rattling of small stones continuing after the main descent had finished. Dust was hanging in the almost still air like dirty gauze.

When the air to some extent cleared, Speke could see that above the now highest point of the rock-slide an opening had been revealed. A sense of vindication swept through Speke, relief after his strenuous efforts. Whether or not there would be any more to be discovered, of course he did not know, but he would sure make it his business to find out. He now fetched matches from his coat.

Some five minutes later he was coming

near to the still unstable, new summit of the rocks and found that the opening that his efforts had created was almost large enough for him to stand upright. Indeed there was a cavern here and many rocks had spilled inside it. Very slowly and carefully he started down inside, much aware that the rocks on which he was descending formed an unstable slope, but eventually he stood on the floor of what was a large cave, perhaps the remains of a mine-working. Speke struck a match.

Even though he had been more than half expecting it, he stiffened when he saw the wagon. They must have taken the horses away. The match died, leaving its sharp tang in the nostrils. By the faint light now penetrating this musty, dust-thick place, Speke moved forward, now able to distinguish the outline of the wagon, and was able to step up on it and bend his head to see inside under the ravaged, hooped canvas. He struck a second match.

Large eyes and a waxen face stared back

at him, making his pulses jump. Ragged hair, a small body: a child's doll. There was a dirty grey, tattered blanket thrown over some objects on the wagon-bed and even before he moved it he knew what he was about to find.

All three bodies were naked, what was left of them, for they were decayed and had also been attacked by rats; a man, a woman and a child. The child was perhaps twice as big as the doll. Though, when he struck a third match he tried to make a closer examination, he could be only reasonably certain that each had been shot in the back of the head.

ELEVEN

Even Speke, long hardened to scenes of death, had been shaken by what he had just seen, and if earlier he had felt anger because of a succession of other events, he had now gone beyond the heat of anger into a mood that some had seen overtake him at other times; a deep-seated fury, outwardly iron-faced, implacable, and it was John Speke at his most dangerous.

So the man, Hagen, along with his wife and child, had paid the ultimate price of unwisely threatening someone with exposure; or at least giving out that he would not rest until he found who it was who had gypped him, and more than that, he had at least some notion of where to start. It was odds-on that this family had ventured nowhere near this unappealing

174

country of their own accord. Who might have driven the wagon out here in all likelihood would never be known. Harry Boland had not claimed to have seen any riders near the wagon, but that did not mean, necessarily, that there had been none. Other men could have been in the vicinity without Boland's having been aware of them, for he had said that he had been angling away and at a considerable distance.

Speke made his way back to the black horse tied beneath the warped lean-to. His next problem was who might well be told of what he had discovered here. Boothby might well be the appropriate man, but having seen at first hand the situation in Sabina between county sheriff and town marshal, and with Speke's personal assessment of Bob Boothby, a question mark had to be hanging over that man. Speke decided that it was a bridge to be crossed only when he got to it. Right now he would head on out of this place and maybe make an overnight camp near the creek where he had rested on the way in.

He was stooping to tighten the cinches when he heard the horses coming. The black's head came up. The horsemen were coming steadily, not quickly, bit-chains clinking. Having shrugged his coat on, Speke now swept it back so that the pistol was reachable, but he chose now to unscabbard the Winchester, then moved slowly to the far corner of the shack.

Because some tall brush was in the way, and a few large boulders, he could see no one, but there could be no doubt that a few moments ago horses had been approaching. Now there were no such sounds. Speke drew back. The day was now well advanced and he had no wish to come up against a number of unknown men in darkness; yet he might be left no option. For Speke was under no illusion that this party, whoever was in it, had entered this particular canyon purely by chance. In spite of attention to his back-trail on the way out of Sabina, he must have been tracked. Maybe for a time they had lost him, then come upon his camp-site, and thereafter cut other sign. And by now, wherever they had come to a halt, they might be able to see the results of his activities at the mine-workings; and assuming that they already knew what the man-made cavern contained, they would not want Speke to leave here bearing that knowledge. Well, he would simply have to take his chances. He backed further away from the corner of the shack and in the next few seconds remounted, but did not scabbard the rifle. There might just be a chance that he might be able to get by them.

Holding the black horse to a walk, he came around the end of the shack, the Winchester gripped in his right hand and tipped back across his right shoulder. Speke's limbs were aching and so was his back, results of his recent labours up on the rock-slide. The black came ambling around some brown, dying brush into a relatively open stretch, and there they were, three of them, all mounted, sitting quietly in line-abreast, spaced about forty feet apart and some fifty yards distant. Speke gently drew the black horse to a halt.

He recognized them at once; Stone, Nickson and Jack Griffin, Griffin not wearing his long duster today, but like the other two, studded leather leggings and grey wool shirt. Speke could discern no weapons in hand, but Griffin, in the middle, was the only one facing him head-on, the others three-quarters angled, the riders' right hands obscured. They sat staring at him for what must have been half a minute before Stone called, 'We *did* want a word, Speke, so we've come.'

'And you've come one hell of a long way,' Speke said, 'to do what you could have got done in Sabina. Cady got you on a short rein?'

'We ain't Cady's servants,' Nickson said.

Speke nodded at Griffin. 'Old Jack there, he is when it suits. And the ginger-whiskered bastard that's right now rotting under six foot of Sabina dirt, he was.' He raised his voice slightly. 'You should've stuck around out there that time, Jack. I'd got but half finished.'

Griffin stared but did not answer, but Nickson said, 'Yuh been pokin' around where yuh got no call to be, Speke.'

So that confirmed that they knew quite well what he had come here for and that indeed they had noticed the opening exposed above the rockslide.

'Easy marks, all three of 'em,' said Speke, 'unarmed and looking the other way. Especially the females.'

At last Griffin spoke. 'John Speke yuh might be, mister, but yuh cain't no ways take all three of us.'

'Then maybe it'll be just you and me that go to Hell together, Jack.'

Nickson, the one slightly to Speke's left, lifted his concealed right hand, a pistol barrel glinting, the other two moving as well now. As Nickson's pistol came swinging up and around to bear on Speke, the man disadvantaged by the range, Speke whipped the rifle down off his shoulder and though the black under him was tending to be restless, flicking and shaking at persistent flies, Speke sent a lashing shot away and saw Nickson punched hard and lifted up onto the cantle as he took the leaden blow.

While the rifle shot was still echoing Speke was hauling the horse around and, gathering speed, went charging away, crouching, weaving among brush, making again for what shelter the shacks could offer, furious shooting erupting behind him, but fortunately for Speke, so far not from rifles. He went plunging in behind the same shack that he had left only a matter of minutes earlier. At best it would provide flimsy cover, and though clearly he had hit Nickson solidly, he well realized the tightness of his situation. These men were hard and unforgiving. They could take their time over nailing him. Speke estimated, however, that there would be about an hour remaining before daylight turned to deep grey dusk, then night fell. Under the lean-to he hitched the black and stood listening but could hear nothing. Likely they were now trying to help Nickson. If Speke had hit him as well as he believed, they were probably wasting their time.

Speke went backing away across the space between two shacks, then looked around him, seeking less obvious cover. Over to his right by some thirty yards was an upthrust of reddish, flaky rock, a beard of sorry-looking growth around its base. Casting glances behind him, he set off at a crouching run and got in behind the rock without drawing either gunfire or shouts from them, wherever they were by now.

Speke spent some time getting himself into a position from which he could see sufficiently clearly, yet still remain reasonably concealed, then waited. He knew that in spite of the fact that Nickson had been solidly hit, they still held the high cards; there were two of them and even though the canyon was fairly wide, they were somewhere between Speke and the way out, with plenty of places for ambush if they simply decided to wait for him to make the next move. And he had the same misgivings as earlier about still being pinned in this place after sundown.

Something caused him to glance towards the rough, reddish-grey wall of the canyon that was across to his right by some two hundred feet. Even as he turned his head a rifle shot lashed from behind talus over there and a bullet came whipping into the flaky rock right in front of him, sending reddish granules flying like birdshot.

Speke went rolling away but as he came around the upthrust his eye caught other movement, this time across to his left and out beyond the shacks, a momentary thing, visible in the gap between two of them. A rifle cracked and lead came punching, searing across the back of his left hand between thumb and forefinger. He had got himself boxed between two riflemen and to get out of the sights of one, he must run the extreme risk of being lined up by the other. They had not missed his move and had split up accordingly.

Pressing his big frame in behind the rock, Speke looked down at his sorely raked hand. Somehow he would have to get a cloth tied around the bloodied mess, but even as the thought came to him the man near the canyon wall shot again, and again granules of rock jumped and distorted lead went howling away to be spent somewhere beyond him.

Soon, one or the other of them would surely nail him, so he would have to take risks, try to get in close to one or the other for just long enough to turn it into a straight shoot, one-to-one, try to cut the odds by half. Setting the rifle aside he decided to close to a range at which his pistolman's skills would be of most use.

He believed that if he tried to get as far as the shacks the man up by the canyon wall would pick him off before he had got ten paces. Going for the man in back of the talus he should be screened from the other for most of the time. The light was fading, though dusk had not yet come down. He could see about sixty feet away a similar, brush-clogged rock, and to get to it he would be running directly towards the man at the canyon wall.

Speke left the Winchester on the ground and, Smith and Wesson in hand, head lowered, went running from cover. The rifleman fired and the bullet nipped Speke's left sleeve as he covered the final few feet, flinging himself down onto his chest as another bullet whacked the ground, spitting dust over him. No shooting had come from the other man and Speke fervently hoped that it was because he was at least for a time out of that man's view.

Speke saw a chance to get another sixty or so feet closer, but believed that he would never make it now by simply getting up and running towards the shelter of what looked like some rusted framework, the remains, perhaps, of an ore wagon whose heavy woodwork was nearly all rotted away, the wreck partly buried under dry earth over which was some coarse, weedy growth. So when he gathered himself, rose and ran on, he blasted the pistol once, then in a pace or two, again, towards where the man was, hoping to have him duck his head, allowing Speke time to reach his new cover.

Speke lay close in to the rusting metal and the small clump of brush growing up through the framework, his breath harsh in his throat, his bloodied left hand fiery with pain. Three bullets came in quick succession, racketing through dry branches, one clanging against browned metal. The rifleman must have been confident of getting Speke now, for he stood up, butt-plate to his shoulder, head canted to one side. It was Stone.

Speke, lying sideways, outstretched, seeking to make of himself the least possible target, saw Stone through the interstices of the branches and took deliberate aim and shot the man. Stone jumped as though mule-kicked, leaping backwards, then screamed as Speke, half rising, shot him again. Then in a dozen strides Speke came to him, knocking the sagging rifle from the man's hands, shoving him down, kneeling over him, pulling away the man's pistol and hurling it from him; for Stone, though hit in the upper left of his chest near the armpit and in the inside of the left thigh close to the groin, was not finished, but was bleeding copiously and making keening noises. Speke took up the rifle, unloaded it and threw it as far away as he could. One dead—as he believed Nickson to be—one severely wounded, one still out there, and the light was turning a dirty grey colour; yet he could still see the shapes of the old shacks. But the black horse had merged with like shadows.

Presently Griffin's voice called, 'Stoney?'

Speke, again long-striding, left the twice-hit, moaning man and headed off towards where, judging by the call, he thought Griffin to be, a place closer, now, to the shack where the horse was tied. That he was right was quite soon confirmed, for a gunshot stabbed the gloom, a pistol, lead humming close to Speke. Speke paused and fired, moving quickly sideways, but no second shot came from Griffin, nor had Speke hit him, for immediately there came sounds of the man running.

Speke waited, standing quite still, working out the direction. Not long after, he heard the sounds of a horse being walked away. Griffin, it seemed, was for the second time in recent days, choosing to pull out while he could still do so, having no doubt read the worst into the screaming from Stone, and his not answering. Speke was wary, though. He could not risk riding out until he was quite certain that it was not merely a ruse. And there was the new problem of Stone, disabled. Speke turned and, still carrying the pistol in his hand, walked back towards where the wounded man was.

When the first streaks of sun came shafting into the canyon, Speke came back towards the shacks leading two nodding horses, the one that had been Nickson's, the other belonging to Stone. Not that Stone would be able to get on the horse much less ride anywhere. Stone was in a sense lucky, however, with neither of the bullets still lodged in him, to be alive. Speke had done what he could for him, which was not a whole lot. He had managed to carry him down to one of the shacks. As well as binding his own hurt hand with a bandanna, he had used Stone's bandanna and strips of shirt to cover the chest wound and to bind his thigh. These measures were quite inadequate but the considerable blood-flow seemed to have diminished of its own accord, and Stone, between the times when he was barely conscious, had had periods of lucidity. Speke had given him water.

'Where's...Griff?'

'Long gone.' Then, 'What's this place?'

'Talley's Camp.'

From the fruitless mining period no doubt. And later, 'I can't get you from here all the way to Sabina. They'll need to send a wagon.' Whether or not Stone could last out that long, should he begin to bleed again, was unknown. But it was not troubling Speke excessively, for the man had been among those who had come here for the purpose of killing Speke himself. So Stone was where he was, and how he was, through his own doing. And Nickson. 'Who was it shot those people?'

Sweat-slick, faint but audible, Stone said, 'Charlie...Redruth.'

Speke thought about it, then asked,

'Whose scam was it? The land titles? Cady's?'

'No...Charlie...an' Griff...'

'But you went along, and Nickson?'

'No... Charlie, he'd go up into Brooks County an' suchlike, on the train...set up the sales...'

'My guess is you and Nickson got a split; and no worries about the law. Cady turned a blind eye?' Almost a nod. Stone was not capable of much movement. 'Boothby? Soderman? The real estate man, Helvig?'

'No...mebbe Bob Boothby, he...kinda knowed. Like, he never said nothin'.' A weak man, Boothby. Harriet had said that and Speke's own observations had soon confirmed it; but Harriet, perhaps, had not been right about Soderman.

'The man Hagen, he must have got a look at Redruth back in Sabina, connected him with the man in Brooks County.'

'I dunno. Mebbe it was jes' chance...bad luck. But he sure sang the song that he knowed *somethin'*. Mebbe...he didn't want to say it...right out, in Sabina.'

'But whatever it was, Hagen couldn't be allowed to leave.' That was not a question, so Stone knew he did not have to gather the strength to find an answer.

Now, in the morning, Speke was heading out. Earlier he had fried slabs of bacon and made coffee, leaving some within reach of Stone, and had left Stone's canteen, and Nickson's, nearby. Nickson's body he had brought back and laid in another of the shacks. He had also retrieved his own rifle and Stone's pistol, loaded the pistol and placed it on the floor near Stone. And he had paid one more visit to the cavern where the dead lay. Then he set out for Sabina.

TWELVE

Washed, shaved, his clothes changed and having had a meal, Speke was again armed with the pistol which he wore on the left side, handle foremost. He had cleaned and properly bound his injured hand, applying an ointment bought from Osborne's drugstore on the way in, the druggist having soberly absorbed Speke's rough condition. One look from Speke, however, had been enough to stifle any comment when Speke had said to him, 'A Sabina man, Audie Stone, is out at Talley's Camp. He's got two gunshot wounds but he was alive when I left him. Somebody best go fetch him in.'

Speke's first impulse had been to visit Boothby and put before him what he had discovered in that place. On reflection he had concluded that in all likelihood Jack Griffin had at least passed through, putting his version of events on record. Speke had not pushed the black horse unduly and had even paused at the old camp near the creek, watering the horse and allowing it to graze. So now it was night again. Now he turned his head, for there had come the sound of footfalls out in the hall. Someone rapped on the door.

Speke drew the pistol and cocked it and opened the door, stepping to one side as he did so. Boothby was standing there, Jeb Cady at his elbow, both armed but their hands hanging by their sides.

Cady said, 'Take it easy, John.'

Speke moved his head and watched them carefully as they walked in. Not until he had closed the door behind them did he put the Smith and Wesson away.

'Osborne come by,' said Boothby, 'about Stone. There's a wagon goin' out.'

'It'll have to fetch Reb Nickson in as well,' said Speke, 'dead.' His stare at Cady drew no comment.

'We got to talk now about what went on out there,' Boothby said. 'Another man dead. That's two...'

'Three,' said Speke softly. 'Nickson, Redruth, Harry Boland.' He crossed to where his long coat had been flung across the bed. From beneath it he drew the child's doll and lobbed it towards Boothby who in a reflex movement caught it. 'As well as one other man named Hagen, one woman and a child. Did Jack tell you only half the story?'

Boothby, his mouth open, was staring at the grimy doll in his hands.

Cady said, 'They're hard men, John. Things happen that aren't easy to keep a hold on.'

'Where's Griffin?'

'Here in town,' Cady said at once. 'Bob here has told him to stay right where he is 'til all this gets flattened out.'

'Jack, he reckons yuh threw down on 'em, on sight,' Boothby said, clearly not knowing what to do with the doll.

'Then he's a Goddamn' liar,' Speke said, looking steadily at Cady. 'According to Stone, your boy Redruth, he had a whole lot to answer for.'

'It's true Charlie could be a maverick,' said Cady.

'So can Jack Griffin,' Speke said. 'Twice, now, he's let fly at me. You know me well enough, Jeb, I'm not about to walk away.' He watched as Boothby went pacing across the room and put the doll on the bed. Both men were obviously on edge. 'Somebody couldn't risk Hagen heading back to Brooks County with a notion of who it was that duped him. Stone says Redruth was behind the land deals.' To Boothby he said, 'At the time, did Hagen come to you?'

'No, he sure didn't,' Boothby said, flushing. 'I never seen the wagon leave. It was here one day, an' the next, gone.'

Cady put in, 'When the woman's brother came here asking, I sent telegrams off, all over, with descriptions. I got some answers, none of them any help. Some places I didn't hear back from.' Speke had already heard this from Wells. It meant nothing. Then Boothby asked,

'Speke, what the hell's your stake in all this?' The way it was put and the way Boothby said it caused Speke to pause before saying anything, but when he did he was looking at Cady rather than at Boothby.

'My sister-in-law, she was mighty concerned about those people. They seemed to drive out of Sabina into nowhere. But we know now it was Talley's Camp, and they were driven by somebody else.'

'Charlie Redruth.' This was Cady, saying it quietly.

'So Audie Stone reckoned.' Then, 'If you'd got your mind made up, Jeb, about our business, I'd have been long gone from Sabina by now and none the wiser.'

Cady's face was tight. 'Just so. Well, it's been worked out now. So we can talk; then there'll be nothing to keep you.'

Speke smiled bleakly. 'Surely the county sheriff will want to hear both sides about the Talley's Camp shoot. Nickson, he's dead. Stone, he'll never be the same man again—if he's not bled to death already. And before I do leave, if I happen to come across Jack Griffin, by God I'll not give him another crack at me. Before you can spit, I'll send him to join Nickson.'

Sharply Boothby shook his head. 'Speke, I can't have no pistolman loose on the streets. It's over. Whoever started it, what the whys an' wherefores was, I got to admit these boys was allers real hard to handle. If Nickson an' Stone was with Charlie Redruth when he shot them poor folks, it ain't gonna be no easy matter to git it into a court o' law. Stories change. An' where's the witnesses? Who's to say what's true an' what ain't?' Boothby no longer sounded like a man obsessed with due process.

'It's been a bad business,' Cady said.

'Real bad. But we've got other matters to see to, John, matters that really brought you here.'

'Indeed,' said Speke.

To Boothby, Cady said, 'Bob, I've got some business to talk with John.'

'Uh? Oh...yeah, well...' But he was still most uncomfortable about Speke. 'I don't want no standoff with Jack Griffin. Folks are jumpy enough as it is, Speke.'

'Why?'

'It ain't the first time yuh've come, so I hear. Ever since yuh come this time, there's been dead to be planted in Sabina. Whether it's all been your doin' or not is beside the point. The sooner yuh git finished here the easier I'm gonna be.'

'I'll ride out when my business is done, and that's mostly up to Jeb.' Speke reached for the child's doll and handed it to the peacekeeper. 'Don't forget this, it's evidence.' Confused, Boothby accepted it and left.

Cady said at once, 'You were talking

fifty-fifty, John. I've got to tell you, plain, it's not possible. I've been through it all with Soderman and his attorney. Given a little time I can raise a third of what the appraisal is. To start with, I can give a signed agreement, based on no further claim. Ever. That's the chance that Harriet's going to have to take.'

'Chance?'

'Well, she could come back here and not have to worry about money, all through.'

'I've told you more than once, she won't come, and you know why.'

Cady went on tautly, 'And if she survives me, the whole damn' outfit is hers, anyway; but not if she takes this way.'

'She could just sit it out, and maybe not have to wait too long.'

'I don't follow you John. I don't follow you at all.'

Speke said evenly, 'It's time to stop shitting me around. I know why those boys have had me in their sights. As soon as I gave out I was coming, somebody took fright. Those two that came after Harriet didn't expect to run into me, but from that minute, they were set on me not coming anywhere near Sabina. There had to be a bigger reason than Harriet. No, Jeb, somebody got the idea I was being paid to follow up that Hagen woman's brother. Then Wells turned up, too. He got a rough welcome; and look what happened to that old man I talked to, Harry Boland.'

'It's all in your head, John.'

'I'll say it again, don't shit me around. Let's get to Charlie Redruth, the lies about him.'

Cady said softly, 'I don't know what in the name of God you're on about, John.'

'I don't believe Charlie Redruth had half enough between his ears to lay out a land deal to anybody anywhere.'

Cady said, 'Well, there's no way you, or anybody, is going to be able to ask him.'

'That's so,' said Speke, 'so I've changed my mind over Jack Griffin.'

'What?'

'I should have asked Boothby to start asking that bastard some hard questions; so that's what I'm about to do now, talk some more to Boothby.'

'I'd leave Jack Griffin well alone,' Cady said. 'You heard what Boothby said.'

'I heard. Now he can hear what I have to say. I've given a lot of thought to Griffin. He's taken more than one shot at me, but in Sabina I haven't seen a whisker of him. Somebody doesn't want me to get any closer than a pistol shot.'

Again Cady said, 'Leave Jack Griffin be. Sure as hell he'd pull an iron. Boothby won't tolerate shooting.'

'I'll put what's on my mind to Boothby.' Speke picked up his coat off the bed.

'You're making a real big mistake here, John. It's time to forget this and take my offer back to Harriet, let this county get on with its own affairs.'

'I can't leave it as it is. I've seen what's out at Talley's Camp.' He could sense the anger that had been building in Cady and believed that if he had been anyone other than John Speke, it would have exploded before this.

They went downstairs, then abruptly, on the boardwalk, Cady said, 'I'll not come with you.' He turned and left. Speke watched the preacher's tall son walking away. Speke walked towards the lighted windows where Boothby would be. Those who saw the big, moustached man striding by were left uneasy. It would be a good thing when this pistolman left Sabina.

Judging by the look on Boothby's face he was not all that pleased to see him either. 'If yuh've come to ask where Jack Griffin is, save your breath, Speke. I've looked, but he warn't where I thought. Don't you go lookin'.'

Speke said, 'Jeb Cady will find him soon enough.'

'What's that?'

'Bob, do what you ought to have done long since; start asking some questions of your own. About land deals. About the

Hagens. They'd been shot in the back of the head. Elney will see that as soon as they're brought in. Charlie Redruth's been named. Convenient, because he's dead. It's a barrel of shit.'

'What the hell are yuh sayin' Speke?'

'Redruth didn't have the brains of a horsefly but we're expected to believe he went up into the likes of Brooks County and sold titles to land, titles that looked genuine. Now, Charlie, he might have done the talking, made the handover and taken the money, but there's no chance he could have worked it all out. For Christ's sake Bob *think* about it. If Charlie used to leave here once in a while, go north by train, who else would usually go, maybe a few days ahead of him?'

Boothby's face was slack and he did not want to meet Speke's slate stare. 'This talk is loco, Speke.'

'I'm putting it in your hands. I'm here to lay information, Sheriff Boothby.'

'You're here to hand me speculation,'

Boothby said, unwilling to concede anything.

'Suit yourself,' said Speke, 'but I've seen Jeb Cady snap before this. I've seen manacled men shot, put down like frothing dogs. When I looked inside that wagon, it was the first thing that came to my mind. I've seen welts and bruises on Harriet Cady's body. I came here for no other reason.'

Both turned as the door-latch clicked. Cady stepped in.

'You look like you've just seen Old Nick,' he said. 'Bob, I've got important things to tell you, things that can't wait.'

Boothby moistened his rather full lips. Speke's eyes had fastened on Cady but with a strange, almost detached interest. Boothby got as far as saying, 'Jeb, yuh....' But Cady held up one hand.

'No, hear me out Bob. And John, it might be as well that you hear this. There's not a whole lot of time. I've been talking with Jack Griffin. Now, I've got to say this: I've had word of some things that have been going on.' Again he raised a hand. 'Oh, I admit I ought to have spoken up sooner, Bob, but it's one thing to hear something's going on and another to prove it. But it's gone too far. When John found that wagon out at Talley's Camp, it changed a whole lot of things.'

Boothby, trying to get a handle on it, said, 'Are yuh tellin' me it was Jack shot them folks.' He had glanced at Speke, but Speke was straight-mouthed, not taking his dangerous slate eyes off Cady.

'Bob, those boys went too far. Jack Griffin's the man you have to talk with, and he's ready to talk. It will get this entire thing put to rest.'

'Jack worked out the land deals? Jack shot the Hagens?' Boothby was still having problems with this.

'The land deals, yes, but it was Charlie killed the Hagens.'

'Where's Jack at now?'

'In Solokow's, a billiards hall in a street off Pitman.'

'He knows yuh've come here?'

'He does.'

Boothby half turned, reached his hat off a peg and put it on. To Speke, he said, 'Jes' as well Jeb come right along here. Now we got us the real story. No speculation.'

Speke stared at him sensing that Boothby was feeling much relieved that now he would not have to confront Cady. But none of it smelled right.

Cady said, 'If you plan on heading right down there, Bob, then as the town marshal I'll cover you, but I'll not get in the way.' And to Speke, 'Best you stay right out of it too, John. Let the elected law handle this.'

On the way out, Boothby hesitated. 'Griffin, is he sober?'

'He's been in the Double Ace and downed a few,' Cady said, 'so best go into Solokow's easy.'

Speke wanted to check Boothby, have him consider more carefully what he was doing. If Griffin was so ready to tell what he knew, then Speke would have expected him to come along to the office with Cady. Slowly he walked out of the office behind them and watched as, first Boothby, then some forty feet behind him, Cady, went pacing along the boardwalk. Because Boothby was who he was, however, he was not able to make uninterrupted progress. From time to time people wanted a word with him.

Speke was standing looking at the general movement along the boardwalk, men and women caught in lanternlight and the lights from store windows. Then Speke craned his neck. At some distance he could still see Boothby but now realized he could no longer see Cady. So the big man went strolling in the same direction, glancing into each of the stores as he went by but saw Cady in none of them. A worm of unease was beginning to crawl in Speke's belly. In his mind he chastised himself for not taking a firm part in what had passed between Boothby and Cady. Now he was trying to recall on which of the streets off Pitman, was Solokow's Billiards Hall. Up ahead of him, the passing crowd thinning, he could see that Boothby had vanished.

Speke went walking on and turned down a sidestreet and had gone thirty yards before he realized it was not the right one and retraced his steps. The next off-street was Adams. This was the one.

That there was some kind of commotion along here was plain enough. Numerous men were straggling away from under a lantern-lit sign that read: SOLOKOW'S BILLIARDS HALL, and they were not wasting any time. Speke half raised a hand, causing a bushy-whiskered individual to fling him a wary look. Speke asked, 'Boothby. Have you seen Bob Boothby?'

'*Seen* 'im? Yeah. He's down to Solokow's right now, come to take Jack Griffin fer murder.'

'*What?*'

'Dunno the whys an' wherefores, mister. I ain't a long-time Sabina man. Seems a while back some folks in a wagon, they got shot, an' now Boothby's come to arrest Jack. Jack, he'd heard he was comin' an' he's sure stirred up. He's holed up in one o' the back rooms. He was all set to light out jes' afore Boothby come.'

'Did you see the marshal there?'

'He's been in an' out. He was there right ahead o' Boothby but I dunno where he got to, 'cause he ain't there now.' The whiskery man went hurrying away.

Speke strode on. Clearly he was the only one going into Solokow's; everybody else was coming out. But Speke had got only a couple of strides inside the main room with its several heavy green baize tables, lamps suspended over each one, when from somewhere near the rear of the building came a thunderous gunshot, then a second one. By the time the second erupted Speke was pounding along a space between big tables at a run, the few remaining patrons and hirelings running for the street doors. Speke had now flung his coat back and drawn the Smith and Wesson.

At the far end of the room, at a door standing ajar, he paused. The tang of gunsmoke was evident, clouding the lamplit passage beyond the door and he could see Bob Boothby sitting against a wall, blood on the floorboards and on the dirty brown wallpaper near him, where presumably he had tried to prevent himself from going down. Boothby was coughing convulsively and liquidly, fingers clawed to his upper chest. The pistol he was carrying was still in its holster. Opposite Boothby was a door that was now closed.

Even in his present awful straits Boothby managed to raise one bloodied hand as a warning to Speke, but Speke none the less came to him and went down on one knee. No more than a glance was needed, though, to confirm that the peacekeeper was in a bad way.

'I'll go get help,' Speke said. 'Griffin still in there?'

Boothby tried to say that he did not know, but coughed, half choked and spat blood onto himself But he did say, *'Cady...'*

'Cady must have told him you were coming to arrest him for murder.' Speke had made a guess at it, based on what the whiskery man had said.

Boothby managed to nod but finally his chin went down on his chest and his breathing had become very bad now. Speke stood up and flung open the door opposite, pistol levelled. Caught in the spill of light from the hallway were some dusty crates and a couple of broken chairs and a sash-cord window, which was raised. Speke fired loudly at a flick of movement outside, gunsmoke clouding the light shafting into the room. Then he ran back through the billiards hall and out onto Adams. Across the street a man lit by the glow from a forge was standing uncertainly in a gateway. Speke yelled, 'Bob Boothby's shot! Get the doc, fast!' Then, 'It's safe to go in.' He did not wait for a reaction but went on around the corner of the billiard hall knowing that to have any chance of coming up with Jack Griffin he would have to risk being seen and shot at from the cover of deep shadows among back-lots and a back street where there were few lights. In his mind, too, was the awareness that Cady had suddenly dropped out of sight, having—so Speke believed—drawn the somewhat ingenuous Boothby onto Jack Griffin's pistol. Griffin, half drunk maybe, had been panicked into believing that Boothby was on his way, not merely to talk, but to take Griffin in for the killing of the Hagens, so in no time at all Cady himself would be distanced from those terrible events. Shrewdly and coldly Cady had used his knowledge of both Boothby and Griffin to engineer this outcome.

As Speke came out behind Solokow's,

fire stabbed in the dark and he felt the breath of lead, but stood and shot deliberately, then moved fast to one side, coming against the twisted poles of a corral. Another gunflash split the night and a corral pole shivered with the impact of a bullet. Speke crouched, having got the instant's outline of a tall man over near some outbuildings behind darkened premises to his right; but this time he did not fire. Instead he eased on inside the corral, which was empty, and went bent-headed across the sandy ground towards where he had last seen Griffin, pistol cocked and extended.

On Pitman and streets jutting off it people were anxious, listening to gunshots. Boothby was shot, either dead or dying—both stories were circulating—and the pistolman, John Speke, was on the prowl. They could hear him. So where in the name of God was the Sabina town marshal?

Speke, ever mindful of small matters which could give a game away, held his left hand behind him lest the white bandage on it betray him, even where there was next to no light. He was still inside the empty corral, down on one knee now, slowly looking all around him. Patience, sometimes, could mean the difference between life and death.

Soon, indeed, patience had its reward. Back along where he had come in, Speke saw the tall figure of Jack Griffin, not where he might have been expected, but out on Adams, limned against the glow of the forge and partly illumined by light from the lantern above the doors of Solokow's Billiards Hall. Griffin had circled to get back onto the street and away.

Until Speke himself, having moved very quickly, was at the front corner of the building, he did not call to Griffin. When he did, Griffin spun about, pistol chopping downwards. What he saw, if only faintly lit, was the big, moustached man, Speke, standing side-on with pistol levelled, before the flash and the jet of smoke came and Griffin was mule-kicked, stumbling backwards, pistol blazing at the sky, Speke walking in, still pointing the Smith and Wesson, firing again, then again as the distance closed between him and the flailing, falling Griffin.

Those who, with Doc Crowther, were just then coming out through the front doors of Solokow's carrying Boothby on a canvas-covered stretcher, the man from the forge among them, were thus thunderstruck witnesses to the killing on Adams. Speke stood where he was, over Griffin, engaged in reloading the pistol.

Boothby was carried on by; presumably to Crowther's rooms. Nobody challenged Speke, but the doctor, pausing to look hopelessly, at the fallen Griffin, said, 'Could be tomorrow before I can be sure about Bob Boothby. This is a shocking business. Boothby claims he was set up, and so was Griffin to some extent. He's named Mr Cady.'

Speke walked with Crowther to the

215

corner of Pitman. 'Doctor, this is partly my fault. I should have gone further, had Cady restrained for some reason...anything.'

'What's about to happen now?'

'I wish to God I knew,' Speke said, 'but I'm on my way to talk with Cady. I'll go to his house. If he's not there, I'll wait for him.' He left Crowther. He had put the pistol away.

Somehow he knew as he made his way along Pitman to Fremont and came eventually within sight of the sprawling frame house, that Jeb Cady would already be there. If Cady had witnessed any of the events on Adams, then slipped away, unseen, then this would be as far as he would run.

In the front yard Speke paused. There was a lamp on somewhere inside. He could see the dissipated glow of it. The front door was standing open. Speke approached but stopped fifteen feet short of it. He could hear voices somewhere behind him, on Fremont, but did not turn his head. Those who had been on hand while Doc Crowther had been examining Boothby in the bloodstained back hallway at Solokow's, had no doubt lost no time in putting around a reason for what they had heard. Among those people would be those who had sided with Cady, those who never got out of line because they were afraid of him; and no doubt those who hated him and wanted to be on hand if he should be about to get some comeuppance. But some of those daring to come to the street, albeit hanging well back, would want to be able to say, afterwards, *I was there when a pistolman, John Speke, called Cady.'* And there would be plenty of others who would say it anyway, who had not been anywhere near.

Speke called, 'Time for you and me to talk again, Jeb.'

After a short pause, Cady's voice said, 'Then come on in, John.'

'No, step out on the porch.' Speke's coat was swept back but his hands were hanging by his sides. After another interval there were stirring sounds, then the shape of Cady materialized on the porch. Speke could see the dull sheen of the pistol hanging heavy in Cady's right hand. 'Never one for an even throw, were you Jeb?'

Cady's teeth shone whitely in the gloom. 'I've been a fool over a lot of things, John, but not to the extent of taking you cheap.' Then, 'Why in God's name did you stick your nose in?'

'I already told you. I had time on my hands. Anyway, I should've known that no matter how much you had, you'd want more. I could have bet on your greed. I ought to have bet on your killing to cover it.'

Cady said, 'The Hepburn posse. Them three bastards, they always stuck in your craw, John. I could see it then and I've recalled it since. You're two men, John. One can stand, like you're standing now, and call me, and the other can preach harder than my old man ever did, and he sure was a Jesus shouter.'

'You can believe what you want,' said Speke, 'it won't change anything. I tried to warn Bob Boothby but he didn't want to hear it. And yes, you're right about one thing: as soon as I saw the man and his wife and the child in that wagon I saw the men with manacles out at that other Godforsaken place.' Then, 'Hagen catch sight of you, did he, while Charlie or Jack was selling him the title? Just a glimpse? Then another, when he came through Sabina? He got to thinking you were in it up to your smile, didn't he? So there was no way he was getting out alive.' In a few seconds, 'You were always a mouthy, good-for-nothing bastard. The preacher's misfire. It didn't surprise me that you'd turn to beating a woman when the mood was on you, then send scum like Griffin and Redruth to fetch her back after she'd had enough and lit out. Not man enough to come yourself.' Only part of it was true, as Speke well knew, but his voice was loud enough to carry to other ears; and it had the effect on Cady that Speke had intended. It sparked a flash of fury, and in that instant, the shrug of movement produced by a paroxysm of rage at being called in such a way by Speke, where others no doubt could hear, gave Speke the split second's signal he had gambled on.

By the time Cady's hand, gripping the pistol, came swinging up, Speke, in one movement, cross drawing and half turning to present a slimmer profile, got the pistol cleared away and across and thundered lancing fire at Cady who, pistol still coming up, was jolted sideways, then came blundering raggedly off the porch, Speke side-stepping lightly, blasting again, hammering Cady against the side of the porch.

Cady, in his bloodied agony, teeth now bared in an awful rictus, still gripped with blind fury, was doing his best to bring the now swung-away pistol to bear on the man he so badly wanted to kill. Speke stood utterly still and shot Cady again, again slamming him back against the porch, then watched as the man sank down, groping in front of him for some kind of support that did not exist, then fell down, dying.

Speke turned and walked away onto Fremont still carrying the Smith and Wesson. Those who had gone ducking for cover were now re-emerging. Someone asked, 'Mr Cady, is he dead?'

'Go take a look,' Speke advised, and added, 'Have him taken away. I'll be back when I've sent word to Mrs Cady and I'll be occupying her house until she can get here. Those that dealt with Cady on matters of rents and leases will have to deal with her now. And anybody that thinks to use that to advantage will have me to deal with.' He strode on, putting the Smith and Wesson back in its scabbard and closing his long coat.

This Large Print Book for the Partially sighted, who cannot read normal print, is published under the auspices of

THE ULVERSCROFT FOUNDATION